FINAL STRIKE

VANESSA M. KNIGHT

Final Strike

Published by Inked Publishing

Cover Art © 2020 by Qamber Designs & Media

Edited by Nancy Canu

ISBN: 978-1-7344206-4-7

Thank you to all the authors that work day and night to put words on the page. Every book is a new journey that inspires me to keep going.

CHAPTER ONE

JULIE CONNOLLY WAS HIDING. She hadn't crouched behind the casket or anything—mostly because there wasn't a casket. But she was standing behind a giant wreath of flowers, watching another random guest walk toward her across the muted green funeral home carpet. Hide was a strong word. She wasn't hiding. She was standing off to the side, giving others access to the urn holding her father's ashes.

The guest stood in front of the burnt remnants of a cold man and cried, dabbing her eyes.

See? Julie wasn't even needed.

She was tired of the platitudes. Tired of the lies. People holding her hand, telling her how wonderful her father had been. What a great man he'd been.

They were trying to be nice. Or they didn't know him. He was the furthest thing from great. He'd told her how imperfect she was every day of her life—too fat, too stupid, too lazy. Too much like her mother. It was only fair she saw him for the ass he was.

Even after he'd ended up in prison, many people didn't see the real him. She was lucky—or unlucky. She'd seen it all.

But the sea of people in the funeral home didn't know. They didn't know their tears were wasted on a man who wouldn't have shed a tear for them.

"You shouldn't be hiding." The nasally voice grated on Julie's last nerve. And that the nasally voice noticed Julie was hiding made it so much worse.

"I'm not hiding." She obviously wasn't doing a good job of it. "I'm taking a moment to breathe. I'm mourning. My father died."

"Yes." Bettina Wilcox—the woman Julie's father had been dating for the last few years—clamped her hand around Julie's arm. Her nails dug into Julie's skin. Perfect black suit dress. Dyed blonde hair pulled taut into a bun, not one hair out of place. Not one flaw.

Except for the fact that she was a raging bitch.

"Your father has died. Show him respect."

"You're hurting me."

"You are representing your family. Your father. Be the gracious hostess you were taught to be." Bettina herded Julie toward the back of the room, where the urn stood on its pedestal.

"I just need a moment for myself."

"No wonder he couldn't trust you to be the executor of his will. You only think about yourself. Please try to remember this is about others, as well. Now go."

Go and talk to people that didn't know her. Or care.

An old family friend hobbled over, all covered in black. Mrs. Smith. Her face was a mask of sadness.

Julie yanked her arm free from her father's grieving girlfriend without too much resistance. Although Bettina's supposed grieving did nothing but cause Julie grief.

Julie moved toward the older woman and further away from Bettina. She rubbed the skin beneath her arm, where she could imagine she'd have tiny bruises in the shape of talons. "Thank you for coming," she told Mrs. Smith.

"I'm so sorry."

Julie wrapped the old woman in a hug.

Mrs. Smith pulled back, still wearing a haunted look. "I just can't believe I'm seeing you twice in one month."

"Me either." Julie had just gone to the funeral of Mrs. Smith's grandson. He was Cody's age. And he had been the center of Mrs. Smith's world. One leukemia diagnosis and two years later, her grandson was gone, and she was destroyed.

Not that Julie blamed her. If she lost her son, she didn't know what she'd do.

Mrs. Smith shook her head, that haunted stare never leaving. "I have to find Bettina. Call me if you or that precious child need anything."

"I will." Julie watched her disappear toward the back of the hall, looking for Bettina—on purpose. The concept was foreign to Julie—like trying to find Hitler. Why bother?

A hand grabbed her arm and Julie almost told Bettina where to shove it. She wasn't hiding anymore.

She was talking. Representing the family as she was taught. What more could she possibly want?

Julie pulled her arm back ready to strike. But instead of Bettina's scowl, Julie's boss and best friend Allison Byrnes stood in front of her. Thank goodness.

Julie practically jumped at Allison, pulling her in for a hug. "Thank God you're here."

Allison let out an oomph. "Are you okay?"

"Bettina." Julie let her go and Allison nodded. If anyone knew the aggravation that was Bettina Wilcox, it was Allison. Julie had shared her personal demon stories enough over the years.

"Just think, after today, you never have to see her again."

"One could only hope." Julie would love to think that she'd never see Bettina again, but she'd never been that lucky.

Allison led Julie back to the end of the line leading to the urn. "Where's your father?"

"In the gold-embossed vase over there."

"They cremated him already?"

Julie shrugged. "Yep."

"That's so Bettina of her." Allison shook her head. "It's not like anyone would want to face him. Maybe get some closure."

Julie heard the tremor in her friend's voice. Allison had been held at gunpoint by Julie's father. If anyone other than Julie needed some of that closure it was Allison—or Allison's husband, who'd actually been shot by the man. Speaking of... "Where's Adam?"

"They're all coming later on. There was a big case they're working and they couldn't get away right now."

The fact that they were even considering coming at all warmed Julie's chest. Policework was always stressful, and they probably didn't need the added stress of a funeral for a man who was nothing but evil to them. "They don't have to come—"

"Are you kidding? They're your friends. Adam is your son's uncle. Of course they'll be here." Allison stepped over to the urn as they hit the front of the line.

"I'll give you a minute." Julie stepped away. The last time Allison saw Julie's father he'd held a gun to her head. She deserved a minute of privacy.

A tear slid down Allison's cheek as she spoke to the urn, too low for Julie to hear. Then she turned to Julie and offered a watery smile.

Julie wrapped her in a hug. "Are you okay?"

"I will be." Allison wiped away the tears as they headed toward the breakroom. "How about you? Did you get a chance to say any last words?"

"Not yet." She'd said everything the last time she'd seen him.

"You should do that..." Allison smiled at someone behind Julie. "I'm glad you came."

Julie turned around, hoping to see one of her friends. But not a friend at all. It was Benjamin Mooring. His dark-blond hair hung over his blue eyes. She knew they were blue. She'd swam in those eyes and almost drowned.

Ben Mooring.

Ex-boyfriend.

Ex-lover

Current co-worker.

Current heartache.

"I'm so sorry for your loss." Ben slid his arms around her. Strong arms. Arms that felt more like home than they should. She blamed the funeral. Funerals were sad. Between the sadness, the frustration of dealing with Bettina, and wishing she'd had a relationship with her father that didn't suck, she was inches away from eating her feelings. Well, eating all the cookies laid out for the guests.

And having Ben this close, holding her so tight after everything they'd been through, was like taking the turns on Space Mountain. She'd taken her son Cody on that ride a couple years ago. It made her head spin and left her gasping for breath.

Déjà vu.

He kept mumbling, "I'm so sorry," and other platitudes. When anybody else said that, it was cold and distant. They hadn't known her or her father well enough to know what she'd lived through. But this man knew it all. He knew more than even her friends knew.

She'd pined after Ben for years before they'd dated. Things had been good once, during the year they spent together. All the hugs they'd shared. All the love they'd had beat against the back of her throat. Her head pounded. Her eyes stung. The ball in her throat grew thicker and heavier.

Because it all disappeared once Ben found out about Cody's father. He'd been cruel. That rollercoaster was on track to do a loop, and she was going to lose her lunch.

Ben's arms were wrapped tight, and she forced her hands between their bodies, pushing against his chest. He must have noticed her squirming, because he let go. Just let go.

Julie's foot snagged on the carpet when she tried to put some space between them. She grabbed onto the nearest thing she could reach, which happened to be the refreshment table. Fabric slipped between her fingers as she landed on the floor.

A tray of cookies crashed down on her head. Coffee spilled over the side of the table. Thankfully it had been sitting out for a while, because it wasn't hot enough to burn the skin—just a bit uncomfortable.

Ben set the empty tray back on the table and kneeled down next to her. "Are you all right?"

All right? Julie stared at the crumbled cookies sliding along her dress. Her hip hurt. Her hands stung. And she was lying in a puddle of coffee. "I'm okay."

"What are you doing?" Bettina hissed in Julie's ear, her hand squeezing Julie's arm, nails digging in to her skin as she pulled. "Get up! If you can't take this seriously, you should just leave."

Tears stung the back of Julie's eyes. This was her father's funeral. Of course she took it seriously. She couldn't just leave. Could she? The crazy in Bettina's eyes stopped her from asking.

"Let her go." Ben towered over Bettina, his face locked in a mask of fierce.

"Mother." One of Bettina's daughters walked over.

Her scowl could've been aimed at her mother or Ben, but more likely it was aimed at Julie. "Don't let her ruin today."

Ruin? It was a funeral. What part was so pleasant that an accident could ruin it? Bettina did release her claws from Julie's arm, and as much as Julie wanted to be thankful to Bettina's Mini-Me, she didn't have time. She had to get away. Away from Bettina and her replicated daughters. Away from this funeral. Away from Ben.

Julie ignored the crumbs clinging to her dress. Who cared if she was covered in cookie? Who cared that she'd made a complete ass of herself? Well, maybe she cared. But there wasn't one thing she could do about it.

She turned on her heel and headed toward the back room where the kids were running around burning off steam. She just needed to grab Cody and she was out of here. Why stay? This funeral was all about Bettina anyway.

If she said that over and over again, she might actually believe it.

In the spacious back room, children ran around on the scuffed linoleum floor and tumbled on the furniture. A babysitter stood guard near the door. "Hi, Mrs. Connolly."

Julie didn't have the energy to correct her. Everyone defaulted to Mrs. when a woman had a child. How could they know it hurt as much as it did? She'd never been a Mrs. Ever. Something her father always made sure she wouldn't forget.

Cody bounced on the couch holding Stuffy Puppy,

a plush tan dog with black floppy ears, as one of the other children bounced next to him. His five-year-old giggle floated around the room, sinking into her soul, a balm for all the wrongs in the world. That sound was her everything. That boy was her everything.

His smile covered his whole face. His cheeks were red, and his golden-blond hair bounced with every jump. His favorite toy knocked him in the head. He was having so much fun.

She hated to steal his happiness. But they had to leave. "Cody."

"What?" He held the back of the couch and bounced.

"Time to go." She waited for him to cry and stomp and pout. Instead, he jumped down from the couch and ran toward her. Thank goodness. She didn't have it in her to fight with another person today.

Julie leaned down to catch him. He bypassed her and ran to the man standing behind her.

"Ben!" Cody yelled, and jumped into his arms. "I was jumping on the couch like at grandma's. And I held on to the back like you showed me."

"Great job, little dude."

When had Ben taught Cody to hold on when he jumped on the couch? Which Cody was not allowed to do. Jump on the couch, not hold on. But Cody knowing Ben well enough to throw himself into his arms—when did that happen?

Cody had been so young when Ben and Julie broke up. She didn't think Cody would remember him. She was wrong.

"Cody, can you grab your coat?" It was the tail-end of spring in Chicagoland, and it shouldn't be cold. But the cold hadn't quite snapped yet.

Ben put him on the floor, and her son ran to a couch by the door and sifted through the coats.

"So I'm surprised Cody remembers you."

"I've seen him a few times when I had to drop some things off at Loraine's." Loraine was Cody's grandmother on his father's side. She was a godsend and more like family to Julie than her father had ever been.

Ben had spent time with her son. She didn't know if that made her want to hug him or punch him. Cody ran to Ben and held up his coat.

Decision made. She wanted to punch him.

How many times had Julie wanted Ben to be there for her? How many times had she prayed he'd come back to her? Too many to count. But he'd been kind to her son. Like now.

Ben slid Cody's little arms through the sleeves. He pulled the jacket around his shoulders and checked the cuffs. He was so attentive as he made sure that Cody didn't get his fingers caught.

Fine. She wanted to hug him. Ben was so good with Cody. Her son talked animatedly about one of his many cartoons and Ben nodded, asking questions. He didn't just pretend to be interested, he actually seemed interested. Almost like he'd watched the show.

"Do you watch Nickelodeon?" Julie asked, curious.

Red crawled up his neck and ears. "Only a few times with Cody."

"Why are you watching TV with my son?" That

might have come out a bit too harsh, but he'd given up any right to her son when he walked away.

Allison walked in the room. "Hey, kiddo."

"Auntie Allison." Cody jumped over to Allison, who'd married Cody's uncle over the summer. Not only Julie's best friend but also family—and Julie's boss, too. She wore many hats.

"I think I saw a swing set outside. Why don't we go see?" Allison swung her stare between Ben and Julie before leading a very talkative Cody out the door.

"So I'm not allowed to talk to Cody?" Anger tinged the fire in his eyes.

"It's confusing for him." For her.

"He doesn't even remember us."

Knife to the heart. Because they never really existed. Wouldn't that be so much easier if that were true.

"I like spending time with him." He slid his hands into the pockets of his jeans as his shoulders slumped. He looked devastated. And having seen how much Cody seemed to light up when he saw Ben—she couldn't take that away from him. Either of them, really.

"Fine. He seems to like you." Taking away something from Cody because of emotional discomfort wasn't in her vocabulary. Her son was first and foremost. "But don't teach him to jump on furniture."

Boundaries were good.

"Okay." He smiled. "We could go out for coffee next week and talk about what I should avoid teaching him."

"I don't think that's a good idea." *Keep putting up those boundaries.* She didn't want a confusing relationship with Ben. She'd loved him and he'd crapped all over it. Oh, who was she kidding—she still loved him. But that didn't change the whole crap thing.

"Why?" He ran a hand along the side of her face, wedging a piece of hair behind her ear. "I think you and I are a great idea."

"We tried that. It didn't work out so well."

"That was my fault." His face held all the regret Julie had felt—all the pain. Julie never regretted her son. But she'd regretted how Ben found out. She should have told him herself. But she was afraid of how he'd react. Which, given his reaction, was founded.

"I said some awful things. You didn't deserve that. But I was hoping..." He was saying all the right things—making her feel all the right feels. But the hurt still lingered. She'd lived so long feeling guilt for everything she did. Ben's disappointment and ultimate disavowing of her was a betrayal she couldn't seem to get past.

But his eyes pleaded. And her heart twisted.

"Julie. There you are." Dale Byrnes walked in the room. Dale, the father of her son. The man who'd disappeared to live in Russia or wherever he went. The man she hadn't seen in over a year. The father who hadn't seen his son in that same amount of time. Apparently he was back. Dale walked over and wrapped Julie in his arms. "I'm so sorry. I came as soon as I heard."

Julie took the hug but wasn't quite sure how to take the *came as soon as I heard.* Dale hadn't even made it to his own brother's wedding to Allison a few months ago.

Ben watched as Dale held on tight. He didn't say anything but the look on his face said he was not happy—jealousy over Dale being so close or from being interrupted, she wasn't sure. But she had a feeling it was a mixture of the two.

"Ben." Dale pulled away. He said Ben's name like a vegan said *steak*. "How are you doing?"

"Fine, Dale." Ben seemed to have gotten the memo, and Dale's name sounded like a carnivore saying *bean burger*. "What are you doing here?"

"I live here. My family is here." Dale nodded to Julie. "My son and his mother. What are *you* doing here?"

Ben's face slowly reddened, and if Julie didn't nip this in the bud, they'd be throwing punches at her father's funeral. The fact that it would ruin Bettina's perfectly laid plans almost made Julie step back and let it happen.

But since Ben worked at Byrnes and Company and Dale's family owned the company, she needed these men to play nice. For the sake of the company. It had nothing to do with her at all. "Ben, can you give us a minute?"

Ben's eyes widened in surprise, but then he nodded.

The nod said it all. He wasn't done. They weren't done. But they were done for now. They were done before Julie did something she'd regret—like tell him she'd give him another chance. Thank goodness for Dale.

That's something she never thought she'd be

thinking.

The second Ben walked away Julie turned to Dale. "I'm glad you could come, but I'm confused."

"Why? I wouldn't miss it. I care about you." Dale ran a hand through his dark blond hair before sliding it in his pocket.

Now she remembered why she'd had a crush on this man for most of her teenage life. He was good looking—everything symmetrical. He had gorgeous green eyes, so caring and kind. Too bad behind that nice package was a self-centered man-baby with Peter Pan syndrome.

Dale tipped his head toward the door. "So, what's with you and Ben?"

Julie wasn't about to go into the headache that was her and Ben. She didn't know how to answer that question for herself, so there was no way she was going to try to explain it to Dale. Even if she could. "Dale, what's going on?"

"What?" His eyebrows were arched in confusion. Which meant he was. He might be a man-child but he was a terrible liar.

"You didn't even go Adam's wedding. Why would you come here for my father's funeral?"

"Well, I wasn't told about my brother's wedding early enough and I had prior engagements. And I'm moving back home, so when I heard, I rushed back. I know none of this worked out like we'd thought, but I'd still like to think we're friends."

She wanted to be grateful. They might not have been the best romantically, but they really had been friends first. And they'd been good friends. Until they hadn't been. But that didn't mean she wasn't going to be nice to him. He still deserved that. He was still Cody's father, if nothing else. "I'm glad you could make it. I'm sure Cody will be happy to see you."

Not that Cody would remember Dale. He'd been pretty young when Dale was last in Chicago, and Dale hadn't really stuck around.

"Me too." Dale studied the bouncing kids. "Where's Cody?"

"Outside on the swings with Allison. Have you had a chance to see my father?"

"I don't need to see him. I got quite enough Edward Connolly when he shot me."

Oh, yeah. Her father not only shot Allison's husband, she'd shot Dale that night too. When her father went over the edge, he really free-fell over the edge. "Want to go outside and see Cody?"

"Absolutely."

They walked in silence. Julie kept her head down, so no one would grab her attention. But even with her head down, she managed to catch Bettina's stink-eye. Naturally Bettina would have evil thoughts about Julie leaving the funeral with her friends. Too bad.

Dale opened the front door of the funeral home, and the cold spring air slapped Julie in the face. She wrapped her arms around her stomach as she walked over to a small swatch of grass with a few swings.

Cody laughed as Ben stood behind one of the swings, pushing him forward. Allison stood off to the side taking pictures with her cell phone.

"You have to show Uncle Adam." Cody pumped his legs as he went higher, one hand clutching Stuffy Puppy.

"Should I send him the picture now, or do you want me to show him when he comes by Grandma's later?" Allison asked.

"Now!" he yelled as Ben stepped away from the swing set.

"Do you want to take over?" Ben asked Dale. That was sweet. Ben was giving Dale a chance to interact with his son.

Dale smiled and jogged over to the set. "Hi, Cody, do you remember me?"

Cody shook his head, but with Allison standing right next to him taking action shots, and Julie on her way over, he didn't seem to mind the new face.

"Do you want me to push you?"

Julie had never heard Dale sound so unsure of himself before. He was usually overly confident of all his capabilities, even if they weren't part of his repertoire.

"Yeah." Cody kicked out his legs and pumped. "What's your name?"

Dale's gaze implored Julie. Like she knew how Dale should answer the question. She shrugged. "Whatever you're comfortable with," she said.

"My name is Dale and I'm your dad."

Cody turned to Dale. Looked him up and down as he stared. Whatever he saw, he tightened his grip on the swing—like he wasn't sure if he should believe this guy, and then he decided he would. "Make me go high."

Dale pushed and Cody laughed.

Father. Son. So cute. Julie stood next to Ben. "That was nice of you to make room for Dale."

"He's his father. I'm not going to stand in his way."

"You're a good man, Ben."

"I'm glad you think so." Ben smiled and pulled his keys from his pocket. "I should probably go. Let you deal with all of this."

"That's probably a good idea." Julie didn't necessarily want him to go, but then again, Ben wasn't really walking away.

Cody held tight and laughed when Dale pushed him a little too high. "Are you really my dad?"

"I am. Is that a good thing?"

Cody swung back and forth, frowning a little while he thought that over. "Are you going to leave?"

"No. I'm here to stay."

Cody smiled. "Then it's good."

He was so easily convinced that everything was fine. Ah, to be five again.

"I wish you didn't have to go." Julie sighed and glanced at Ben.

He was watching the Norman Rockwell family moment with a pensive expression. "It's better this way. You three need to figure things out."

"You're probably right." Of course, he was right. That didn't change the fact she didn't want him to go. But it was a selfish wish.

"I'll see you in the office."

"Yeah."

"Julie." Bettina's oldest daughter poked her head out of the door to the funeral home. "My mother wants to see you."

Julie nodded. "I'll be right in."

Allison leaned over, stopping her photo shoot. "Are you going back in?"

Bettina's daughter disappeared inside. The door closed. The door to her father, his disappointment, Bettina, and everything else clicked closed too.

Cody jumped off the swing, stuffed his dog in the crook of his arm and grabbed Julie's hand. "No," Julie whispered. "Let's go get ice cream."

She walked to her car with a light heart and a new beginning.

CHAPTER TWO

A FEW DAYS LATER, Julie sat at her desk outside Allison's office. Life had somehow moved on. Her father was in an urn somewhere with Bettina, and Julie had no intention of fighting her for it. Those two deserved each other. Both angry. Both evil. Both out of her life. She hadn't heard a peep from the woman.

And that was okay.

"Why are you here?" Allison's heels clicked across the tiled floor.

"Because I work here?" Julie should really start looking for a nursing job. She'd been slogging through night classes for over a year so she could help others. But the money here at Byrnes and Company was too good. She wanted a nest egg for when it was time to take a pay cut. And that nest egg was almost where she wanted it to be.

But she hadn't quit yet. Unless Allison wanted to fire her. She'd joked about that a few months back, to motivate Julie to find a nursing job. But she hadn't meant it. Had she?

"I know you work here, but I told you to take the week off." Allison sighed.

Oh yeah, that. "Cody's in school and I can only clean the house so many times." Not to mention study so much anatomy. Or create so many flash cards.

"What about homework?"

"Ugh." Julie's head hit the desk. She folded her arms over her head, hoping to keep out any more talk about school. "No more studying. My brain is full. And it doesn't keep my mind off anything."

Allison pulled a guest chair over from against the wall. "Speaking of. How are things going?"

"Fine, I guess. Loraine brings us dinner every night." Julie lifted her head, her forehead stinging from where it smacked the desk. Loraine was Cody's paternal grandmother. Allison's mother-in-law. She knew how awful Julie's father had been and treated Julie like a daughter. Gave her access to the guest house on her property and offered free babysitting. She was another godsend.

"She wants to make sure you eat." Allison sat next to Julie's desk and leaned back in the guest chair.

"She asked me last night what I wanted for dinner tonight. So I guess I don't have to cook. I'm not complaining, but I feel bad."

"Don't feel bad. Her cooking is epic. And she loves to do it."

"And it gives me time to just be with Cody at

night." Julie sighed. "Sometimes I forget how much time my classes take away from him."

Allison smiled. "He's a good kid, and you're doing a great job."

Julie wanted to smile, but her mouth wouldn't cooperate. She never knew what to say to compliments or praise. Her life hadn't exactly been flush with either.

Allison stood, and put the chair back near the wall before coming over to lay a hand on Julie's shoulder. "I'm heading out to a client meeting in a few minutes, but I'll be a call away if you need me."

"Thanks."

Just as Allison went into her office, the desk phone rang and the elevator opened. A man in a suit stepped out. Crap. Not any man. Ben.

If Julie thought he looked good before, he looked amazing now. Dark blond hair brushed the collar of a black suit. Blue eyes. He carried a box in his hands. A box with ribbons. Maybe a gift.

He had to know she couldn't be bought with gifts—although she did like them. Which he knew. Which she hated that he knew. He wasn't allowed to know what she liked. Not anymore.

He set the box on the corner of her desk. "This was being delivered when I walked past the security desk. It's for you."

Not a gift. From Ben. Part of her was happy he hadn't resorted to cheap bribery. Part of her wanted a gift. What? She didn't get many gifts these days.

The nondescript white box didn't have the usual

scuff marks or postage—just her name and the company address. "Who's it from?" Ben asked. "Boyfriend?"

It was none of his business who it was from. She had no boyfriend, or friend that was a boy. Or even prospects. She was over thirty, overweight, in college, the mother of a five-year-old—so she answered honestly. "I don't know, but not a boyfriend."

"Good." He smiled. "Are you going to open it?"

"Yes." She stood up as she turned the box over, but didn't tear at the tape. It felt private. It was her package. Not Ben's. "Don't you have somewhere to go?"

"Nope." He smirked as he leaned his hip against the desk. "I can leave if you need to be alone."

The anticipation was killing her but so were her nerves. She didn't want to be alone with this. "Fine."

Tearing the tape, Julie opened the box, revealing a letter from her father's law firm. She ripped that open and scanned it—the gist of it was this was what her father left her. Great. Part of her hated he'd left her anything. Another part was happy for any scrap of attention her father was willing to give.

She lifted another letter and a shiny wooden box out of the open package. Julie slid her index finger over the intricate loops of her name on the envelope, in her father's distinctive handwriting. She could picture him writing. Maybe wanting to make amends. Regretting their relationship. Wanting them to be close. Maybe she'd misinterpreted their last interaction...

And then she read the letter.

· · ·

FOR SO MANY YEARS, I've blamed myself for your incompetence. For so many years I've wondered what I could have done differently, but your mother's blood runs through your veins and there wasn't a thing I could do to remediate the situation. But despite our shortcomings, there is still hope for Cody.

My estate is prepared to give you two hundred and fifty thousand dollars to extricate yourself from his life. Bettina will raise him. She has agreed to provide guidance for his aptitude for languages.

You never could follow a direction, but I'm hoping you will see the benefits to this arrangement. You will no longer be a single mother. You can continue to focus on yourself, without the guilt of ignoring your son. You can move on and know that Cody will be in the most capable of hands.

AT THE BOTTOM was his signature. Just his signature.

Her vision stumbled over the letter. Again. And again. It wasn't the mention of incompetence or her mother's inferior blood. She'd heard that her whole life. She was used to all of that. But Cody?

"What the hell?" Ben's voice from behind Julie made her twitch. Somehow, he'd moved, and she could practically hear him reading the letter.

She turned the piece of paper over. The paper that held all her father's contempt for her. The paper that offered to pay her to leave her son's life, because she was somehow such a train wreck of a mother that she didn't deserve to have him.

Maybe she didn't. He was an amazing kid. Smart. Maybe Bettina would do a better job with all of the languages her son was going to speak. He picked them up so easily. A friend in class spoke Spanish, and now so did Cody.

"I can see your mind racing. Don't." Ben came around in front of her and lifted her chin with two fingers. It was so gentle. "He's wrong. Your father doesn't know you and he doesn't know Cody."

"But he's right. Cody is special." She turned her head away from Ben's hand. She didn't want to see the concern in his eyes. Every look made her think he cared.

"Anyone can see that. You just have to meet Cody to know he's brilliant. But he has teachers to help with languages. He has you to love him. He needs that. And Bettina's ice heart could never compete with what you have to offer."

Julie couldn't hide the smile. He was right. Cody was a child who needed his mother's love, not a commodity to be managed. Her father would never have understood that.

The man actually thought she'd take the money and hand over her son. Was he crazy? Of course he was crazy. She undid the clasp on the wooden box and tipped up the lid. Her father's pocket watch. White gold. She clicked it open, revealing a small piece of paper with Cody's name and a note. *For my grandson.*

She raised the watch to her face and inhaled. It

didn't smell like him. She couldn't feel her father from holding the watch. She couldn't hear his voice. So why it made her feel twelve again, she had no idea.

"At least the old man left Cody something."

"I don't want anything." And she didn't. Nothing he could give her wouldn't be tainted somehow.

Ben smiled. "Then you won't be taking that money and hitting the clubs?"

"I'm a regular club rat." Laughter rolled through her chest as she shoved the letter and the watch away. "How will I survive?"

He raised his hand to the side of her face, just a ghost of his finger as it slid along her chin before his hand dropped to his side. "You'll survive. You don't need his money or anything else. You're the strongest women I know."

She didn't feel strong, but she couldn't help the glow in her chest from his words.

"How about that coffee?" His breath was mint and heaven—and oh so close. She could lift to her toes and be close enough to kiss him. Close enough to taste him.

Julie remembered the last time he'd asked her out. At the funeral. She'd told him it wasn't a good idea. It still wasn't. But right now, it was easier to play dumb and play with fire. And he was fire. His body was hard against her and her blood flamed. All her girly parts were howling like a tea kettle on full boil. She blinked at him. "Coffee?"

"The one we talked about the other day."

"I believe we agreed it wasn't a good idea."

"You agreed." He leaned toward her. His lips

hovering over hers. "I would never agree that time spent with you was a bad idea."

Julie sighed as he leaned down. She knew she should stop this. She knew she should run. But her lips tingled in anticipation. She—her heart, her body—wanted this. She just needed to get her head on board.

BEN SLOWLY LEANED IN. He wanted to give her time to say no. He really did. But part of him wanted to hurry before she got the chance. He stopped a breath away. He could practically taste her.

Her eyes closed. She wasn't pulling away. She wasn't running. He bridged the distance.

Her lips were soft. He loved the feel of her lips. And he'd forgotten how much. Until now. A ghost of a kiss. He wanted to deepen it, but he wasn't going to scare her away. He missed more than just this. He missed talking to her. He missed touching her. And he'd do anything to get that back.

He pulled away. "Dinner?"

"I can't tonight." Her voice came out in a breathy burst.

He knew that feeling. And he'd made her feel that way. "How about tomorrow?"

"I have class. Wait. No, it was cancelled." Her teeth worried her lower lip. He'd like to worry those lips between his teeth.

Allison cleared her throat. "I'm sorry to interrupt, but we need to be on the north side in twenty."

"Okay." Ben wanted to tell Allison he had to wait for Julie's answer to his question. But since she was his boss and one of the few people who'd given him a chance when his life imploded a few years back, he had no intention of yelling or telling.

Although a glare might have been pasted on his face. He was only human. "We'll talk later?" he asked Julie.

"Yes."

"Yes, we'll talk later or yes to dinner?"

"Both." Julie's lips pulled into a smile. And dammit if that wasn't contagious as hell.

"Really?"

Allison walked over and leaned in. "Take the win and shut up," she told Ben. To Julie, she said "We have to go. He'll pick you up tomorrow night."

Ben didn't want to leave, but Allison was right, they needed to leave. Now. "I'll text you and we'll figure out where we want to go," he told Julie as he jogged to the elevator behind Allison and got in. The doors snapped closed.

"So where are you taking her now that she finally said yes?" Allison knew all about Ben's epic crash and burn with Julie. Hell, one of the reasons Julie was anti-Ben was because he'd tried to take over Byrnes and Company back in the day. And he might have overreacted when he found out Dale Byrnes was the father of Julie's son.

Colossal mistakes. One after another. He'd lost his job, and Julie. Somehow Allison forgave him, though.

She'd always been on his side. Even when she didn't have to be.

Ben shrugged. "I was going to take her to Duffy's."

"Duffy's? Like, bar food and peanuts on the floor?"

"Yeah, it's where we had our first date." The elevator doors flew open and they stepped out into the atrium, nodding and smiling as they passed a spattering of employees. Even though Byrnes and Company owned the building, they only occupied a handful of floors, so there were a lot more unknown than known people.

"I'm going to go out on a limb here. And don't take this the wrong way." Allison's heels clicked as the two of them crossed the tiled floor. "When you first started dating, you probably hadn't pissed her off, right?"

"No." That hadn't happened till much later, when he'd lost his damn mind. Once through the revolving door, the spring wind sliced through the jacket of Ben's suit, leaving him cold. Like this conversation.

"She was probably easy to impress back then, because you didn't have two years of crap to make up for." Which made sense. Allison raised her arm and a taxi pulled up to her toes. Between Allison's blonde hair and stunning physique, she was a taxi magnet.

Julie was amazing too. And Allison had a point. He had to come up with something more impressive if he wanted to be the lucky guy who took her home. He could go expensive. "The Chop House?"

"Julie won't care about expensive." Allison slid all the way across the back seat of the taxi, making room for Ben.

"Then what's wrong with Duffy's?" he asked, getting in next to her. "It has nostalgia on its side, if nothing else."

Allison shook her head. "If you're looking for a place with great wings where your feet crunch walking to the table, then Duffy's is for you. But if you're trying to have a romantic dinner, go with something more."

"Something more what?"

"Just more. Nice. Quiet. Romantic."

Julie didn't talk to Ben about much, but back when they did talk, she mentioned that she didn't get to go to grown-up restaurants. A toddler throwing a tantrum tended to ruin the ambiance.

"The Club Room over on the north side?"

"Like that." Allison pulled a stack of papers from her bag. "We should probably talk about this meeting. The teacher's union wants to keep giving something to their retiring teachers. But they can't afford the watches and brooches they've done in the past. If we can come up with something else that meets their needs, it could be huge. It's a big contract."

"Imagine that. Retiring is popular." Ben had thought about his own retirement a time or two. Not that he was anywhere near that stage in his life. After all the fallout a couple years ago, he'd taken a year off to get his priorities back on track. And he hadn't really thought about it since he'd gotten back to work. One of those priorities he needed back on that track was Julie. Which was one place his mind should not be. But no matter how much his brain should be on this presentation, he couldn't get his mind off her.

She'd finally said yes. He finally had a chance to get to her listen. To get her to forgive him. Or at the least start forgiving.

He just had to make sure dinner was perfect. The night was perfect. He was perfect.

No pressure.

CHAPTER THREE

JULIE HADN'T BEEN able to concentrate on one thing this afternoon at work. Not since she'd said yes to dinner tomorrow. What was she thinking? Easy answer. She wasn't thinking, not after that kiss.

But she didn't do dinner. Okay, she did dinner every night. But she didn't do dinner with a man, with Ben. Not since he threw her stuff out of his house and pulled a Houdini from her life.

He'd been mad that she hadn't told him about Dale being the father. Well, not even Dale had known back then because of her father's brand of crazy. There was no way she was going to tell anyone else.

Even if it had been the man she'd loved.

Loved. Sometimes she thought she'd gotten over all the feelings. Then she saw Ben and everything rushed back to the surface. The warmth from his stare. The pulse of desire from feeling him close.

Thinking of warmth and desire while she was picking up Cody at the ice rink wasn't going to win her parent of the year. So she ignored the excitement of their upcoming dinner. And she avoided any thoughts of Ben and what could happen after said dinner—her body parts tingled just a bit. They hadn't gotten the whole *ignore it* memo.

She tugged open the glass doors to the rink. The cold from inside the building slapped her in the face, freezing any tingly parts. It reminded her why she was here. And why she needed to focus. Her son would be practicing, and she'd get the third degree afterwards—did she see his shot, did she see when he skated from one side of the ice to the other. A quiz on how well she paid attention.

And if she didn't, the hurt in his eyes would be too much to bear. So she watched and smiled and reveled in how much he'd learned over the past year.

Her shoes sank into the rubber flooring in the main hallway. She dodged children and parents as she made her way along the scuffed Plexiglas lining the rink and climbed the creaking bleachers overlooking the ice.

Skate blades scraped. Children screamed. Hockey pucks slapped against the wooden wall lining the ice.

She scanned the children playing, looking for Cody, but they were all covered in coats, hats, and even some scarves. Cody had grown up on the ice and attending games, so he never wore the layers. Which made it more strange that she couldn't see him skating with his class.

Loraine was supposed to pick up Cody from school and bring him to hockey. At least that was the plan. Maybe she hadn't made it in time. Julie pulled out her phone to text her. Loraine always called if she couldn't take Cody to practice. Always.

"Mrs. Connolly," a voice called from the ice.

"Ms. Connolly." She tried to smile, but why bother. Didn't anyone realize how embarrassing it was to correct the whole Mrs./Ms. thing? It was like a big sign that blinked "Not Married".

"Sorry." The barely twenty-something smiled. He didn't know how embarrassing it was—he was practically a kid himself. "Ms. Connolly, Cody is in the office with Coach. He asked if you can head on back when you got here."

"Is everything all right?" She stood and walked toward the edge of the bleachers, waiting for him to answer before she broke out into a run.

"Cody's fine. I think there was an incident."

Incident? That didn't sound fine at all. She wanted him to define *incident*. She wanted to jump on the ice and grab the kid by the jersey and ask him to explain. But throttling children—even teens—was generally frowned upon. And who knew how much this kid even knew.

She needed to see Cody. Count all his fingers and toes. And the only way to do that was the office. She jogged—or attempted to jog in heels and a skirt— through the throngs of people to the coach's office, which was behind the locker room.

Although locker room was a bit of a stretch. It was a line of lockers behind the bleachers. There was no privacy and barely any room. Although it did have the locker part down.

The smell of ice and sweat permeated the air and made it impossible to breathe as the door to the coach's office got further and further away, like a cruel funhouse mirror. She dodged one child after another, not to mention their hockey-stick-length bags on the floor, all of them trying to keep her from her son. Parents stood around and talked, mostly ignoring the kids as they sprawled on the ground pulling on skates or swapping them for gym shoes. And miraculously ignoring the woman jumping over their children's heads with high-heeled daggers on her feet.

Julie sped through the chaos to the battered wooden door at the back. She knocked and immediately turned the knob. She didn't have patience for an invitation. The coach sat at his desk, and Cody sat at a table coloring in a book.

"Coach."

"Miss Connolly, I'm glad you're here."

"Mom!" Cody dropped his crayon and ran to her, wrapping his arms around her waist.

"Hey, kiddo." She held on to him a little too long. This was like being called to the principal's office, and she had no idea what she'd done wrong. "Is everything okay?" she asked the coach.

"Yeah, Cody's fine. Please have a seat." He waved a hand at the chair in front of his desk.

"Cody, why don't you finish coloring that picture, and I'll talk to Coach."

Cody pulled away and sat at the table, picking up the crayons and carrying on as if nothing had happened.

"We had an incident today with a woman." Coach leaned forward, eyeing Cody before he continued. "I was working with a few of the students and Cody was on the bench. A woman with brown hair started talking to him, asking him questions. When we approached her, she left."

"Do you know who she was?" Even as she asked the question, she knew it was dumb. If he knew who the woman was, this probably wouldn't be an issue.

"It wasn't anyone we've seen before." He shook his head and frowned. "Cody, why don't you tell your mom what that stranger lady wanted."

"She said she knew my mom." Cody kept coloring and didn't look up. "She wanted to know if Mommy was coming to get me, and if I came to practice every day."

"And what did she ask you about school?"

"She asked if Mommy picks me up every day or if she works."

"And did you answer her?" Julie prompted when Cody didn't answer. There was no way Cody would have answered her. Right? The way this conversation was going, she had a feeling he answered. How many times had Julie gone over stranger danger with her son? Yet, here they were.

From the look on Cody's face, her tone might have been a little too harsh.

"What did you tell her, sweetheart?" You caught more flies with honey, and caught more children doing something wrong with a sweet tone.

Cody's eyes brimmed with tears. "I said you work downtown and sometimes come and pick me up."

"Did you know who the woman was?" Maybe Allison came down to the rink and started asking him random questions—and changed her hair color. Seriously grasping at straws here, but that was better than outright panic. Right?

"No." He shook his head, eyes widening. She could almost see their conversations about stranger-danger flashing in his head.

She wanted to wrap him in her arms and tell him not to worry. But she was pretty fricking worried. He was talking to strangers. Strangers asking weird questions about her.

"So, she was a stranger?" The coach didn't appear to care that Cody was upset. He got right to the point. Honestly, he might be right.

Cody gulped and nodded. The realization that he talked to a stranger must have sunk in. So had the danger. "I didn't mean to talk to her."

"We know, but you need to be more careful." Julie nodded. "Did she ask anything else?"

Cody shook his head before dropping his chin to his chest. He wiped at his face with one wrist and sniffled.

"You did a good thing coming to talk to me," the coach told Cody, and stood up. "You were very brave telling us what happened."

Cody still sniffled, but turned his red eyes the coach's way. "I was?"

"Absolutely." Coach kneeled in front of Cody and gave him a high-five. "And now, you're not only brave but smart, too. You know to never talk to anyone you don't know. Never tell any stranger about your mom or you. You know that if anyone comes up to you, you're going to —what do we do when a stranger comes to talk to us?"

"Run away and get an adult."

"Another high-five." Coach held up his hand and Cody smiled as he slapped it. "That's right."

Cody nodded. The tears seemed to have dried up.

"And you know to tell us if a stranger talks you. That's the brave thing to do."

"Yep."

A smile tried to form on Julie's lips. The coach was handling this like a champ. Not reprimanding. Not yelling. Letting Cody learn from his mistakes without punishing him further.

If she wasn't so worried about what this meant, she might actually let the smile break free. Someone was way too curious about Julie's comings and goings. Someone who Cody didn't know. And Cody knew all her friends.

What that meant, she had no idea. But she had a feeling it wasn't good.

THE NEXT DAY, Julie sat behind her desk at work. Ben was out with Allison schmoozing potential clients. The phone hadn't rung—much—so she had her pharmacology textbook open wide. And she really was trying to study drug interactions.

But all she could think about was dinner. Tonight. With Ben. Should she leave work a little early to make sure she was ready when he came to pick her up at six? She was nervous and excited and the combination was exhilarating and…and nauseating.

The elevator dinged. Which meant someone was coming. Not that she cared. Not that she stopped looking at her book and stared at the doors that crept open, hoping it was Ben. That would be pathetic. So she definitely wasn't doing that.

The metal doors inched open and a suit leg appeared. Ben. A smile turned up the corners of her lips. And then the whole body appeared. Not Ben.

"Good morning, Dale." She forced the smile to stay on her face. Nothing against Dale, but his inability to be there for Cody made her want to cry for her son. And his inability to be Ben made her want to stick her nose back in the book. But that would be rude.

"Morning." He came up to the desk. "I missed you this morning."

This morning. Dale had taken up residence at his mother's house. Not that she'd seen him all that much. Neither had Cody. She could barely understand how he didn't see Cody when Dale was living overseas, but how could a man be a deadbeat dad AND live in the same house? There had to be some kind of counter-prize for that. She kept her smile steady. "I had to get Cody to school, and then I came in here."

"Yeah, I bet it takes a while to get him ready." Dale

played with the pencil holder on her desk, staring at the red pen he kept pulling out and pushing back in.

She wanted to mention how he could get up early and help her, or that maybe he should know how long it took to get Cody ready for school, but it wasn't her place... Wait. Yes, it was. "If you'd like to get him ready for school sometime, I'm sure he'd enjoy it." Not to mention it would give her time to get ready at home instead of blow-drying her hair using the open car windows as she sped down the Eisenhower Expressway.

"I'll try." Which in Dale-speak meant never. He'd tried to be a boyfriend back when they'd slept together, but she'd never been enough for him. He'd been back on the party circuit before their second date. He'd tried to stick around when he found out he had a son, but his wife pulled him back to Russia. His kind of trying was trying for all of those he tried for. On top of that, he wasn't a morning person. Or a responsibility person.

Thankfully, the phone on the desk rang, saving her from explaining how much she hated when he said he'd try.

"Good morning, Byrnes and Company. This is Julie. How may I help you?" Part of her hoped Dale would get the hint and go on with his day. But the shadow looming over her desk said otherwise.

"This is Ralph Pederson. I'm your father's lawyer." He had that serious cold-hearted voice. This guy and her father were probably besties. If he had a bestie. It was probably more like they drank scotch and counted their money together. "I wanted to see if you received the contract from your father?"

Contract. He said it so nonchalantly. Like she would willingly sign over her parental rights. Casually give away her flesh and blood.

"I've received the contract."

"Good. Have you signed it?"

"No." There was no point dragging this out. "I'm not going to sign it."

"May I ask why?" He actually sounded confused.

His confusion confused her. "No." She wasn't playing any more of these games.

"This is a good opportunity for your son."

"Yes, Cody is *my* son. And I will decide which opportunities are appropriate." Julie held the phone so tight, she was surprised it didn't crack.

"But—"

"This is not up for discussion. Please don't call me again." She slammed the phone down and dropped her head onto the desk, the open textbook cradling her face. Her heartbeat roared in her ears and she almost forgot she had an audience until he spoke up.

"Is everything okay with Cody?"

"He's fine." She didn't want to get into specifics with him.

"That didn't sound fine."

Her head popped up from the desk, face heating. She didn't care. This was her problem. Her son. He hadn't been around enough to earn a vote. "It doesn't matter how it sounded. I have everything under control for my son."

"Our son." Dale stepped back. "I just want to know if there's anything I can do to help."

The breath stuck in her lungs chose this moment to gush out. He sounded so sincere. He just wanted to help. And wasn't that sweet? It wasn't his fault her father was a control freak who thought she'd give up her son at the drop of a hat. Or for a quarter million dollars.

It wasn't Dale's fault her father didn't love her the way a father should love a daughter. None of this was anyone else's fault. And getting mad at him wasn't the answer.

"I'm sorry. It's been a rough day." Well, it hadn't been until she'd gotten that call. "That was my father's lawyer. But it's all taken care of. It's done." At least she hoped it was done. She said no, the money would go somewhere else and her life would move on. And her father would never have influence over her again. Either way, she wanted to leave it behind her. "Why are you in the office today?"

Dale smiled. He obviously didn't mind the topic change. "I came in to see if there's anything I can do. I want to get back into the swing of things. Is the office at the end still vacant?"

"Yes." Julie smiled. "I'll tell Allison you're here when she gets back."

"Thanks, Julie." Dale reached across the desk and rested a hand on hers. "It will all be okay."

"Thanks, Dale." She smiled but she didn't really feel it.

Logically, she knew things would be okay. Her

father and his bullshit were behind her. His particular brand of crazy was gone. Logically, all of that made sense. But as a daughter, his disappointment still stung. She still felt his annoyance. She still heard his voice questioning her every move.

And it would take many hours of therapy to truly put all of that behind her.

CHAPTER FOUR

BEN OPENED the car door and got out. He wore a suit every damn day. So why the tie around his neck felt like a noose, he had no idea. This dinner with Julie was his chance to make everything right. He should be celebrating as he stepped out of his red Prius and clicked the locks. But instead of feeling excited, he felt like the lunch he hadn't finished was about to revolt.

He'd sold most of his clothes when he took a year off to find himself. A year to figure out what he wanted in life. And somehow money wasn't his driving force any longer. Italian suits and expensive shoes didn't hold the allure they once did. But the Berluti loafers on his feet were so comfortable, he couldn't give them up. It was the one thing he'd kept from his "before" lifestyle.

Up the long driveway was a garage, just behind the main house on Loraine's property. Ben followed the winding path that started next to the garage, walking past the pool area until he was surrounded by trees.

He'd never been back here. Never had a need. He'd

been to the main house to drop off plans or documentation for Loraine. But he'd never had the guts to come out back to the guest house and see Julie. Until tonight.

And his guts were still on full mutiny as the little house came into view.

It was cute. A white single-story cottage with brown trim and flower boxes hanging from the windows. That must have been Loraine's doing. Julie's thumb was almost a charcoal black, since she tended to kill anything with roots. Not that she didn't try. When he'd bought his last house, she'd offered to take care of the plants along the front.

It was the offer that counted. Not the line of dead plants.

Enjoying the tranquility, he almost missed the bike tipped over on the walkway. Cody's bike. God, Ben missed the little guy. He missed Cody almost as much as he missed Julie. Almost.

He knocked on the brown door. Silence. No movement in the house. No movement outside. Maybe she changed her mind. Maybe she'd never intended on going out with him. Maybe there was a zombie apocalypse he didn't know about.

If there was an apocalypse, he had more problems than being stood up. Somehow that didn't put the silence into perspective.

Julie smiled as she walked around the side of the house, dandelions spilling from her hands. "You're early."

He checked his watch. Shit. "I am early."

"I haven't had a chance to get ready." Her short

brown hair was clipped back and hung in wisps around her face. A small smudge of dirt lined her chin. Her cheeks pinked as he watched her.

"You're beautiful." And he meant it. She was.

She ran one hand over her hair and sighed. "I'm a mess. We were picking flowers."

"I picked the most." Cody ran around the house with his own ball of dandelions. He held open his hands as dandelion heads and stems fell to the ground. "Look how many I got."

"Great job, little dude. Good thing I didn't bring flowers. I don't think I could compete."

"You can have some of mine." Cody shoved the flowers in his hand. Flower goo and dirt clung to Ben's fingers as Cody abandoned his trove.

"Thanks."

"Are you going to Grandma's with me?" Cody bounced on his toes now that the heavy flowers weren't holding him down. He kicked and spun. "I learned this from Donatello."

"That's awesome." Ben used his free hand to attempt a karate chop—one that made contact with his face, bouncing his head backward. "Ouch."

His ineptitude had the desired result, and Cody laughed. So did his mother.

"You're doing it wrong," Cody told him. "Do you want to watch Teenage Mutant Ninja Turtles? They do it best."

"I would love to, but I need to eat dinner."

"You could eat dinner with me and Grandma."

Cody always had the answer. He was an amazingly sweet kid.

"I have plans, little man."

"With who?"

Ben had no idea how to answer that. He wanted to shout from the rooftops that Julie agreed to have dinner with him. However, he didn't think she'd like him announcing that to her son.

"Me, sweetheart. We're going to dinner." Julie jumped in, and Ben could admit the fact that she owned their date made his heart beat a little faster. The smile she threw his way made his pulse jump.

Cody's lip quivered as he pouted. "Can I go?"

"It's a work dinner."

Ben didn't want to be hurt by those words, but they delivered a knockout punch to his heart. Logically, he knew she was just trying to talk her son out of wanting to tag along. But that wasn't the only reason she told Cody it was a work dinner, was it? She didn't want Cody to know they were dating.

Made sense to protect him. But damn, did it hurt.

"Let's go inside and get ready for Grandma's." She opened the front door and held it open for Cody and Ben. "Wash your hands!"

Cody disappeared around a corner that looked like it led down a hall. The inside of the house matched the outside. Warm and inviting. A light brown couch sat in the main living area, facing a tan stone fireplace with television hanging above it. Light filtered in through the multiple windows lined with off-white drapes. A cream rug sat in the center of the room. How that rug stayed cream with Cody running around, Ben had no idea.

The kitchen was small but opened to the living area. Pictures of her and Cody and a wooden *Blessed* sign created a homey vibe.

Water came on down the hall. Something clunked.

"Don't mind the noise," Julie said. "Cody's washing his hands."

Water splashed and sounds ricocheted down the hallway. Ben could see Cody in the bathroom, standing on a small stool and fighting with a Donatello soap dispenser. "Will your bathroom survive?"

"Probably not." Julie came closer, so close Ben could smell her perfume—unless she naturally smelled like happiness and lavender. She shifted her focus down the hall. Her son flailed and water went everywhere. "Do you mind waiting a few minutes while I get ready?"

A few minutes? He'd been waiting months. A few minutes was nothing. "Not at all. Can I do anything to help while you get ready?"

"No. Have a seat. I'll be right out."

"Mom, I'm gonna bring your iPad?" Cody stood at the end of the hall, body angled to the right. His shirt was soaking wet and dark with dirt.

"Do not go in my room," Julie called out.

Cody's shoes slammed against the hardwood floor until he was back in the living area. "But I wanna take it to Grandma's and show her the picture I colored for her."

Julie sighed, but managed a smile. She always had a

smile for her son. It was one of the things Ben loved about her. Just one.

"Of course, you can take it, but—" Her tone stopped Cody in his tracks. "I will get it from my room. I want you to pick out a shirt to wear tonight."

"This one." He tugged at the shirt he had on, adorned with nunchuck-wielding Teenage Mutant Ninja Turtles and the aforementioned mud.

"Pick one that's not covered in dirt and water."

"Fine." He stomped back down the hall and turned to the left.

"He'll probably come out before me. Are you okay sitting with him for a few minutes?"

He couldn't control the look that came over his face. And he knew there was a look. She asked the questions like he hadn't been around kids—that kid— most of the child's young life. He'd practically helped raise the kid. A few minutes alone was nothing.

She dipped her head, her lips tipping up at the edges. "I'm sorry. That was a dumb question. I'll be out in a few." She walked out of the living room and down the hall, disappearing to the right. Ben distinctly heard a door close.

"I have to show you." Cody ran back into the room, book pages flailing.

"That looks like an awesome book." Ben sat on the couch and Cody climbed up next to him. His little body leaned against Ben's chest. Blond curls wedged under Ben's chin.

"This one's my favorite." Cody turned the page as

Ben held the book. "You're my friend." Cody nuzzled closer and smiled.

Tears poked at the back of Ben's eyes. "You're my friend, too." This kid. What was he doing? If this didn't work out with Julie, she'd never let him near this kid again.

His heart broke just thinking about it.

HOLY CRAP, what was she doing? Getting ready for a date. With Ben. Okay, Ben was the part that made her insides all squiggly and giggly. Ben was in her house. And from what she'd heard, he was probably reading a story to her son. Her ovaries might explode.

Through the sliding glass door that led from her bedroom to the back porch, Julie watched the sun disappearing. It would be a cool night. She could wear a dress, as long as she wore nylons or something to cover her legs.

She really didn't have time for a shower. She needed to get hot-date-cute before Ben decided it wasn't worth it and he ran away. She wrapped her hand around the knob to the closet door. Weird. She didn't remember closing it this morning. Then again, she couldn't remember what she had for breakfast.

Her cell phone vibrated on her nightstand. She'd left it there during their trip through nature. If she brought the phone with, Cody would beg to use it. If she accidentally left it back at the house—oops. Not really an oops. It was more fun to watch all the critters they'd found and pick the silly flowers. He'd been so excited, he actually forgot about touchscreens for a while.

None of that helped with her current predicament —what to wear for the man who got away and had been a total jerk but was now back looking hotter than ever and reading to her son, making her ovaries crackle. Was there an outfit for that? Hallmark probably made a card. Why didn't The Gap make an ensemble? Maybe they did.

Her phone vibrated again. Darn it. She abandoned the closet and checked her phone. Allison.

Good luck.

Ride that man like a bologna pony. Git along little doggies!

Julie typed *What?* Good luck made sense, but bologna pony? Had Allison lost her mind? Julie knew her friend was Team Ben, but...

Another vibration. *That was Brook. Ignore her. Good luck. You be you and have fun.*

Ah, Allison's sister, Brook. A lawyer and friend, who was completely devoid of a filter.

Makes sense. Thanks. Julie dropped the phone on her bed. Where was she? Ah, yes. She needed clothing. A complete overhaul. Julie opened a dresser drawer, pulling out a new pair of underwear. Sexy red getting-lucky underwear. Yeah? No. She tucked them back in the drawer. This wasn't a date like that. It was a getting-to-know-you-again date.

If she wore that little sliver of satin, she'd be way too tempted to show them off. And she was tempted enough as it was. She still found Ben ridiculously hot. Which was an unfortunate thought as she took off her clothing alone in her room...with the ridiculously hot man down the hall.

She looked in the mirror at her naked body. She wasn't a complete mess. She'd managed to stay out of the mud Cody had doused himself in. Thank goodness. A little bit of lotion and a nice dress and she'd clean up real nice.

Julie stepped into the stomach-holding, never-to-be-seen-by-anyone panties. Safety in granny-panties. After pulling, prodding, and briefly writhing on her bed to get the waistband over her hips, she was appropriately sardined and ready for an outfit.

She whipped open the door to her closet, and a black-hooded battering ram came at her. Her arms flailed. She grabbed for their arm, but her fingers slid off the black cotton jacket.

Down. Down she went. Whoever it was left the closet and moved toward the sliding glass door.

No. Julie grabbed the intruder's left leg with one hand. Not enough. She clamped on with both hands, and her body banged against her dresser. Everything on top of her dresser fell to the floor. Bottles slapped against the wood and shattered. Her fabric jewelry box slammed into her shoulder. Julie flinched, and the intruder pulled away. She kicked her legs to get closer.

Yank. The body dropped to the floor with a groan. A deep groan.

The criminal's right leg barely missed Julie's face,

skinning her neck. She pulled back as that right leg tried another pass. Dammit.

"Stop!" Julie gasped, struggling to roll her half-naked body over both legs and pin them down. The criminal's shoe caught on the thigh-band of her Spanx. The bad guy jerked like a landed fish, and Julie finally angled her body over their legs, pushing them to the floor.

Another groan.

The bad guy wiggled. Julie held on. Her breathing erratic. Her heart beating out of her chest. "Why. Are. You. Here?"

Julie's bedroom door vibrated with a knock. "Is everything okay in there?" Ben sounded concerned. He should be. Julie was holding down a bad guy. Not that he knew that.

She almost called out for help. She almost told Ben to come in.

"Mommy?" Soft knocks on the door. "Is everything 'kay?"

Dammit. She couldn't let Ben in here. Not while Cody was in the house. There might be more intruders. There might be someone with a weapon.

"I'm fine. Ben, please take Cody to his grandma's and call the police."

"Are you sure you're okay?"

"Please get him out of here." She tried to hide her groan, but she had to keep the bad guy here, at least until Ben could get help.

"I'll be back in a minute." Ben must have heard the strain in the words, and she appreciated that he was trying to hide it from Cody. Thank goodness. "Let's go see Grandma, buddy."

As soon as she heard the front door close, Julie asked the squirming mess on the floor, "Who are you?"

The person underneath her surged, and made it halfway to their feet. There was no way Julie could hold on to them. Legs scrabbling, Julie launched herself at the intruder. Stars danced in her eyes when a foot banged the side of her head.

The intruder threw open the sliding glass door and ran out. Julie's bedroom door flew open, and Ben followed the black blur as it disappeared between the trees.

Julie tried to stand and fell back on her butt. Head spinning. She touched her temple and stared at her bloody fingers.

She crawled to the bed and picked up the phone. *Cody.*

She needed to talk to Cody. She hit Loraine's picture and waited as the ringback tone chirped in her ear. Long rings that went on forever and ever, never-ending and low.

Please answer. Please answer.

This had to be the longest call in the history of calls and no one had even answered on the other line yet. She got to her knees, head spinning. *Cody.* She needed to hear his voice. She needed to know he was okay.

Loraine's voice came over the line. "Are you okay?"

"I'm fine. Where's Cody?"

"He's watching TV. Ben told me to call the cops. They're on their way. What happened?"

"There was a break-in."

Loraine gasped. "I'll be right there."

"No. Please. Stay with Cody. I'll come by you as soon as I can."

"I'll wait, but you call me if you need anything."

"I will." Julie clicked end and stared at the screen, long after it went from wallpaper to black. Where was Ben? She wanted Ben.

As if he heard her, Ben jogged back into the room, shutting the sliding glass door behind him and locking it tight. He was covered in sweat and leaves. And none of that mattered as he kneeled down and wrapped his arms around her. "Are you okay?"

"I'm okay now," she said into his chest, muffling the wobble. At least she hoped it did. Even if it didn't she was moving her head. Ben's chest was firm and warm. His hand on her back kept her from spinning into oblivion.

"Do you know who that was?" he asked.

"No." The house was quiet. Everything was quiet. The calm after the storm. Sirens blared in the distance. The cops were on their way. Maybe it was more the calm before the storm. Because somehow a storm was brewing, and she was smack dab in the middle of the eye.

CHAPTER FIVE

A FEW HOURS LATER, Julie sat on one of the padded couches on Loraine's back porch and watched the police walk through the yard toward her little house. Cody was asleep in his bedroom upstairs with Dale watching over him. Julie originally fought Loraine over remodeling one of the rooms for Cody, but Loraine insisted. Now Julie was pretty glad she'd let it go. Cody was able to sleep through all the drama.

Julie wanted to sleep through it, too.

"Are you okay?" Loraine sat down next to Julie on the bench, laying her hand on Julie's knee.

"As okay as I can be."

"Maybe you should sleep in the house tonight."

This was like having a mother there for comfort. It was what Julie imagined her mother would do, if she was still alive. "I'm not letting someone scare me out of my house."

"And I understand." Loraine's fingers wrapped around Julie's. "But I don't want you or Cody to be in danger. One of Adam's friends is going to set up security. And we'll have guards for the next few days while they set up the system."

"Then I'll be fine."

"You may be fine." Detective Shay Washington walked onto the porch, cop uniform of slacks and dress shirt nowhere in sight. She almost looked relaxed in her jeans and T-shirt. Almost.

"Aren't you outside your jurisdiction?" Julie asked her. They'd gotten to know each other over the past few years—first when Shay questioned her during the murder investigation that led to Julie's father's incarceration, then when they went on a trip to Las Vegas for Allison's bachelorette party. Now, they were friends who hung out whenever Julie could get away from school and work and mommying.

Shay ran a hand through her short black hair. "I'm off tonight, so when Adam called Garret to set up security around the house, I thought I'd come by and see how you're doing." Shay's brown eyes lit at the mention of her boyfriend, Garret. It was too cute seeing no-nonsense Shay with googly eyes for the man she loved.

"I'm fine." Julie's hand instinctively went to the bandage on her head.

Shay sat on the couch across from Julie and leaned her elbows on her knees. The woman was always ready to jump up, never leaning back to relax. Although it could be that she didn't want to lean back on the gun strapped to her hip.

"Shay, would you like a drink?" Loraine patted

Julie's hand and stood. "Let me get you girls something to drink. Lemonade?"

"I'm okay, Loraine." Julie wasn't exactly in the mood to drink, even something as simple as lemonade.

"Nonsense. I'm going to grab a glass for myself. Would you like some?"

Julie nodded. "Sure."

Loraine drifted to the back door and walked inside. Her husband died a few years ago and life had moved on for her family, but not so much for Loraine. It was sad. She was way too young to seem so frail.

"You and Cody could spend the night at my place if you don't want to worry about all the noise around here." Shay nodded to the police officers yelling across the yard.

"I'm not backing down. More than likely it was just a random robbery gone wrong."

"Why do you say that?"

Julie shrugged. "I'm normally at school on Tuesday nights. I wasn't supposed to be home. Someone probably knew that and thought they had an easy target." She laughed. "Not that I have anything worth stealing."

"Was anything stolen?"

"I think we came home before they could get anything." Julie couldn't help the relief that flooded her. Now that everyone was safe, she could honestly be glad that nothing was taken. She didn't have a lot of money to replace the necessities. And there were some things she could never replace. Her mother's wedding ring. Her grandma's china.

"Maybe." Shay watched the cops walk back and forth on the path that led to the cottage.

"You think it's something else."

"I'm not sure." Shay got up when Garret appeared from between the trees.

"Hey Julie, how you holding up?" Garret smoothed back his blond hair before leaning in to kiss Shay.

Julie would like to think that if one more person asked how she was doing, she'd scream. But she probably wouldn't. Her friends just cared. Cared enough to be outside stalking her house this late at night. Yeah. She couldn't complain. "I'm okay."

She brushed her temple. The medication she'd taken was wearing off. The cut hurt, but the EMTs had ruled out concussion—the only reason she wasn't on her way to the hospital. So that was positive.

Today had been pretty crappy. She'd take any positives she could get.

Loraine came out carrying a tray. "I brought enough for everyone." And she had. Somehow, she'd poured more than three glasses. It was like she knew what people needed before she even knew they were there.

"Where are you staying tonight?" Garret looped his arm around Shay's shoulder just as Ben walked up.

"She's staying with me," Ben said.

Since when? Julie wanted to tell Ben not to be so presumptuous, but the guy looked exhausted. He'd been running around since he'd knocked on Julie's door earlier, and hadn't had a chance to breathe.

"I'm staying at my house," Julie said.

Ben sighed. "There's glass all over your bedroom. You'll still need to clean that up before you can go back in."

Picking up glass and vacuuming. Not fun. She was just as tired as Ben.

"I can start on that," Ben offered. God bless him. But there was no way she was going to keep him here any longer than he had to be.

"No. Don't bother." Julie leaned back, defeated. She didn't want to let the bad guys chase her out, yet here she was. Wondering where to go.

"You can stay here." Loraine picked up one of the remaining glasses of lemonade and handed it to Julie. "I have extra rooms, and then you can be here if Cody wakes up."

"What about Dale?"

Loraine laughed. "I think he fell asleep in the chair next to Cody's bed. But a boy always wants his mommy."

"Thank you so much." It was the right choice. The logical choice. "I'd love to stay tonight."

"We still have some work to do in the house," Garret said, "and then I'll have security on the grounds. Ben is going to take the first shift while I brief the guys."

"If you or your men need a place to stay, I have plenty of room." Loraine sipped her drink, sadness coating her gaze. "Or Shay, if you want to stay here, we'd love to have you. I'm just so sorry this happened."

"This isn't your fault." Julie leaned into Loraine, wrapping an arm around her shoulders. "You've been so amazing through all of this. Thank you for letting me stay."

Loraine attempted a smile, but something was keeping the sparkle from her eyes. "You're always welcome here. I should get to bed, though, if you don't need me any longer."

"Get some sleep." Garret finished his lemonade and slid the glass onto the tray. "Julie, the police are just wrapping up. If you want to head in to bed, I'll make sure the house is locked up."

"Is there anything in the house you need right now?" Ben emptied his glass and put it on the tray next to Garret's.

Her whole world had been violated. Shoved off its axis. Slowly tilting with no stopping. She wanted familiar. She wanted her stuff.

But she was an adult, and saying she wanted to cuddle her stuff wasn't high on the adulting list. She'd been half naked when the cops arrived, and managed to grab some clothes. Enough to get through tonight and tomorrow. She could get through a day of work and school... School. "Can you grab my school bag? It should have my laptop inside."

Thankfully she'd made sure her homework was done so she could go out on her date—the date that didn't happen.

Ben nodded. "I'll text you when I have it."

"Well, that's settled. Let me show you to your room, dear." Loraine went to pick up the tray.

"Let me get that for you." Julie got to it before

Loraine. It was the least she could do. "Thank you, everyone."

"Good night. We'll be here if you need us." Shay grabbed Garret's hand and headed toward the path to Julie's house.

Ben nodded and followed them.

Loraine's smile was tired. "Don't you worry. Between Garret's security team and Adam's cop friends, this will be the safest yard in town."

"I'm sure." Julie knew deep in her heart this house was safe. Adam, Shay and Garret would make sure of that. But that didn't stop the unease gripping her throat. It didn't stop the fear.

Julie left the tray on the counter in the kitchen and followed Loraine upstairs. Knowing where her room was—knowing her friends were outside keeping guard —knowing Cody was in the next room—none of that made a difference. She'd never sleep tonight.

Verdict was out on whether she'd sleep again for a while.

***

AN HOUR LATER, Ben watched the last of their friends recede from Julie's house. Having their friends around helped, but having all the cops around made him nervous. The last time he'd been involved in this much police activity in Illinois, he'd been a murder suspect. He hadn't liked it then and he still didn't like it now.

He'd let the cops lock the door with the promise to

stay out. But Julie needed her laptop. Ben was going to get it.

Inside the front door, he flipped on the light. Everything looked the same. The living room was untouched. The kitchen quiet. The only difference was the police tape hanging from Julie's bedroom door.

Failure gripped his chest. He was in this room when Julie was attacked. What if she'd been hurt? What if he hadn't gotten to her in time? Scenarios flashed before his eyes in an involuntary horror show.

His heart sped as fear crept up his spine, giving that beat a straight shot to his head, echoing in his skull. He could have lost her. He would have lost everything. The realization about knocked him on his ass.

Julie's schoolbag wasn't visible in the main part of the house. Dammit. That meant her bedroom. Or Cody's. But why would she keep her bag in there?

He made his way down the hall and turned on the light in Cody's room. No bag. But there was something Ben recognized. Stuffy Puppy. The stuffed dog with floppy ears lay in the middle of the floor.

That dog went everywhere with Cody. In all the excitement, he must have forgotten it. Ben picked up the dog, turned off the light, and slipped across the hall to Julie's door.

It was closed, and covered in police tape. Maybe the bag wasn't in here. Maybe he wouldn't have to do the limbo to get inside. He pushed the door open and reached around into the room to turn on the light.

The room was a mess. Everything that had once probably sat on the dresser was now splattered across the floor. Glass shards sparkled on the floor. The room smelled like a brothel. Jewelry sat in puddles of perfume and lotion. This cleanup was going to take work. Thank goodness Garret said he knew people.

Julie's school bag sat in the center of the bed. He'd seen her walk around the office with it all the time. Which meant now he was going to have to get under the yellow police tape. Or over.

Either would be a challenge. The cops had gone a bit nuts. Six times across the door. Six times. Like one or two strips wouldn't get the point across.

Ben stuck Cody's stuffed puppy in his shirt and dropped to his knees, sliding underneath the lowest strip into the bedroom. There went that theory. He apparently hadn't gotten the point with six strips of tape, so the point was obviously not made. Not that any amount of tape could keep him out. Getting to his feet, Ben avoided the worst of the mess on the floor and grabbed the bag.

Just as he turned around, someone said, "Ben?"

He hadn't heard anyone come in. He hadn't heard a sound. But the gun pointed at him and the voice in the doorway told him someone was here.

Ben didn't move as his eyes refocused on the man behind the barrel of the gun. "Garret. You scared the shit out of me."

Garret's lowered the gun. "What are you doing in here?"

Ben raised the bag. "Schoolwork."

"You're not supposed to be in here."

"Neither are you."

"I came in when I saw the light."

Garret had him there. Ben had been the one to turn on the light. He hadn't thought about the security roaming the grounds. He should have. Because there was a chance Garret wouldn't let Ben out of the house with this bag.

"Julie needs her school bag for class tomorrow. It's not like it has anything to do with the intruder."

Garret looked at him, and everything in Ben said he was going to give him a hard time. Garret might be a friend, but this was a police investigation, and while he might not be a cop, he had that police mentality. Hell, he was practically married to one.

"Don't tell anyone you came in here." Garret eased the police tape out of the way to let Ben through. When they were both in the hallway, Garret put the tape back up again. When he turned to Ben, he frowned. "What?"

"I'm just surprised you're helping me."

"Why?" Garret thumped Ben on the back. "We've been through a lot. And I never really did get a chance to pay you back for making sure Shay wasn't hurt in Vegas."

Vegas. It had been fun—except for the part where some guy tried to knock out Shay and Julie for their jewelry. Ben had been there and had chased the bad guy away. "You would have done the same thing."

Garret nodded. "I would have. But I wasn't there. You were. I appreciate that, man. Anyway, after all Julie's been through with her dad dying and now the break-in, she doesn't need any more setbacks."

"Thanks." Ben reached in the bedroom and turned off the light.

"Is that all she's going to need?"

Ben checked inside the bag. Notebook. Laptop. All the things she'd pull out in the lunchroom when she'd take time to study. "Yeah, this should be it."

"Good. I'm sure they meant to take this down before they left, but I'm not touching it just in case."

"Nope." Ben hiked the bag onto his shoulder and started toward the front door.

"How about Cody?" Garret called out.

"What about Cody?"

Garret smirked as he pointed to Ben's chest, where Stuffy Puppy's nose stuck out from the collar of his shirt.

Ah. Yeah. Didn't everyone carry stuffed animals in their clothing like a kangaroo? "Stuffy Puppy."

"I have yet to see that kid without that, so it's a good thing you grabbed it."

Ben nodded, relieved Garret wasn't going to make a big deal out of it. "Let's get out of here before someone else notices the light on and we have to start creatively explaining." He followed Garret out of the house, hitting the living room light before shutting and locking the front door. "Thanks for everything, Garret."

"You too, Ben." He disappeared between the trees.

Darkness enveloped Ben as he headed along the winding path to the main house. Crickets chirped. Wind rustled the trees and brought with it a cold nip. That cold slid up his neck and gave him a jolt. Not enough to keep his eyes open, but enough to remind him that he needed to go.

All of the events of the evening pushed down on his eyelids. It had only been about five hours since he'd shown up to pick up Julie, but somehow it felt like fifteen. He needed to get this stuff to Julie and make his way home. He had over an hour's drive and less than that in his reserves.

CHAPTER SIX

THE BEDROOM WAS QUIET. Dark. But nothing Julie did would shut off the noise in her mind. Between the excitement of her almost-date, the fear of the break-in, the annoyance at the disruption in her life, she'd managed to feel all the feels in one night. Which sounded exciting, but really it just made her want to hurl.

She got out of the ridiculously large bed. It had to be a king. The room was bigger than her living room. Large Victorian furniture—dresser, armoire, night tables—all matching the four-poster bed.

If she was at home and couldn't sleep, she'd pull out her homework. But she didn't have her homework here. Ben said he'd grab it, but who knew how long that would take and she was bored now.

He hadn't come back. And since he lived over an hour away, that probably meant he'd headed home. And why wouldn't he? If she could head home, she'd be all over that. There was nothing keeping him here. Not one reason for him to stay.

Part of her hoped he'd left—back to the whole distance to his house. But part of her wished he'd come and say goodbye. She wrapped her arms around herself, but her arms didn't warm her up. Didn't make her feel safe. Wanted.

Her body didn't hold all the magic bottled in Ben's arms.

Her cell phone jumped on the dresser—or maybe that was her that jumped. The screen lit the ceiling as Julie made her way across the room.

You up? Ben's words lit up her phone—and other places of her body. He hadn't left.

Yep

Come down and let me in.

OK

She looked in the mirror above the dresser. She couldn't see much with only the light from her phone, but she saw enough. Her hair was a mess. She was a mess. She ran her hands hand along the sides of her head, figuring if she couldn't comb her hair into submission, she could at least pretend.

Cody's room was silent when Julie went out into the hall. From Loraine's room came the soft hum some television show. Most nights she watched TV until she passed out. Which meant she wouldn't hear Julie skulking around the house

Julie shuffled down the stairs in the dark. Her toe bumped against the side table that stood in the front hall. Even though Julie had been here many times over the years, she didn't know it well enough to navigate in blackness. She fumbled with the locks on the front door, and after much under-breath swearing, she got them open and there he stood.

The moonlight lit him from behind. And he looked good. "I think I have everything you need for school." He lifted the bag in his hand.

She opened the screen door and took the bag. It felt right—smooth fabric and frayed handle.

"Do you want to check it before I leave?" Ben asked.

"Sure." She stepped aside. "Come on in."

They walked through the house to the kitchen. Julie hit the light switch and laid the bag on the granite island that had to be as big as her house in the backyard. "Can I get you something to drink?"

He yawned. "No. I should probably go."

With the light on, she could see him clearly. Bags under his eyes, whole body drooping. "You shouldn't drive like this."

"Drive like what?"

"Tired."

"The longer I stay, the more tired I'll get."

"I could make you a cup of coffee for the road." She attempted to smile, but the words she wanted to say next stole the curve of her lips. Because if he said no... "Or maybe you could just stay here tonight."

"I don't know..."

That was pretty damn close to no. And she couldn't handle being turned down by him again. She'd been turned down for many things in her life, but when that rejection came from the man she loved—that was a new level of hell. "Let me get you some coffee, then."

"I want to stay," he whispered, like he was a teenager sneaking into his girlfriend's house and didn't want to wake her parents.

Since they were adults—and she was definitely not his girlfriend—that was ridiculous. Not that she'd take it back.

"Then stay," she whispered back.

"Is that a good idea?"

"Probably not, but I have a huge bed. And I don't want to sleep alone."

He stepped closer, maybe to hear her better or maybe he just wanted to be near her. She chose to believe the latter.

"I don't know if I can do that," Ben said, still whispering.

He didn't know if he could stay with her. Why would he want to? She'd spent the past year pushing him away—too afraid to let him in. He had to move on at some point. Too bad he chose to move on when she needed him most.

"I get it." She would not cry. She would not let him *see* her cry. Just... no crying. She pleaded with her tear ducts to stay dry. They were always overachievers. Heading to the fridge, she opened the door. Anything to distract herself. Her mind. Her eyes. "I'll make you some coffee for the road. Do you want cream or sugar?" The cool air felt nice on her over-heated skin.

"No."

"Okay." She shut the fridge and stared at the coffeemaker. She should press start. Get this over with.

"I meant no to the coffee." He touched her arm and she wanted to melt into those pile of tears she was holding back.

She sighed. "You really shouldn't drive this late at night without some caffeine or something."

"Let me ask you something."

"Sure." She opened the cabinet and stared at the mugs on the shelf. They were black, with the Byrnes and Company logo—like all the mugs at work.

"Look at me." Ben's voice was soft.

She didn't want to. He felt sorry for her. And why wouldn't he? Her life was a telenovela, and not in a good way.

"Please."

The please got her. She couldn't say no.

"Why do want me to stay?" Ben asked when she finally faced him. His words were filled with an emotion she couldn't name. Sadness, maybe. Fear? But no pity.

If she told him the truth, would that change? Would he walk away again, leaving her alone? They'd built up a quasi-friendship over the past year. She didn't want to lose that. Then again, she couldn't be just his friend. It was too hard.

"Why, Julie?" Her name on his lips almost did her in. How many times had he whispered her name in reverence? How many times had she'd prayed she'd hear him do it again?

She licked dry lips. "I want you here with me."

"Me, or anyone?" How could he not know? Before she could say anything, he continued. "I can't do this if you just want someone and not me."

"I've always wanted you." *You just haven't always wanted me.* She kept that last piece to herself as her heart twisted. She didn't want him to change his mind. "Stay with me. Just sleep."

"Fine." He shut the cabinet before reaching for her hand. "Let's go to sleep."

She followed him up the stairs and prepared for a night of sleeping with the man who owned her heart.

THEY'D REALLY JUST SLEPT. The whole night. Which wasn't a surprise, since Ben's eyes shut before his head touched the pillow. He'd been that tired. So had Julie. Given it was almost eight and she was still asleep.

Her body was warm and soft beneath his hand. They'd pulled the old she-slept-under-the-covers and he-slept-over-them. Highly unnecessary after the drama of last night, but somewhat welcome this morning. Even with the blanket, he could feel the warmth of her body. Her soft hips. The dip of her waist that led up to gorgeous breasts.

Her body was full and gorgeous. Even after she lost the weight, she hadn't lost the hourglass shape that was all woman. And the blood pumping through his veins said he liked it. Not to mention the blood pumping to other areas. He eased his body away from hers.

He didn't want to explain that he indeed did not have a pencil in his pocket and he was actually happy to see her—and feel her—and stroke her. Not that he was stroking her, exactly. It was more his hand moving slightly, wishing it could stroke her. Which was not helping his psyche and the whole blanket-between-them thing.

He stopped moving his hand and his body, taking a moment to enjoy her in his arms. Again. He never thought they'd be here again. He never thought she'd forgive him. Not that he didn't have more groveling to do, but he'd do it. He'd do anything to get her back.

He could hear the pounding of little feet outside the door. Cody was up. Loraine whispering through the door about no running in the house told him she was up watching the little guy. Which meant Julie could sleep for a little bit longer.

"What time is it?" Her groggy voice broke through his thoughts. So much for sleeping a bit longer.

"Eight."

"Shit." She threw her arm over her face and sighed.

"Loraine is watching Cody. I heard them in the hall." He leaned over and slid kissed her cheek below her arm. "You have time before you have to get up."

"I wish." She sighed. "I have to get Cody to school and hockey, and then I have to get to the hospital."

"What's at the hospital?"

"I'm on shift for my clinical today."

"How long are the clinicals?" He hadn't realized she'd gotten far enough into the major that she was already working at the hospital as a nurse.

"Today is eight hours."

An actual nurse helping people get well. "How long is school and hockey?"

She smiled and it just made his heart melt. "School is till two-thirty. I take a late lunch to pick him up there and then drop him at hockey."

"Why don't I take him and pick him up? I don't have any meetings this morning. And you should focus on the hospital."

She rolled over and looked at him like he'd just asked her to shove a boot up her nose. And he hadn't. He didn't think he had.

"You don't have to take him."

"Why not?" He twisted a finger in the blanket covering her chest. He wanted to pull it down and wrap himself in her, but they were moving slow. Only sleeping. And he was going to stick to her rules if it meant getting her back—even if it might kill him.

"Ben, I don't want to confuse him." A crease formed between her eyebrows.

"I'm not saying we grope each other in front of the kid. I'm saying I take him to school and hockey. I swear I won't speak to him. I'll drive him Miss Daisy style. Or if that's not good enough, I could put him in the trunk if it would feel less personal."

The crease flattened as she laughed. Success. "It's not that. I don't want him to know you stayed here."

"He's five. He doesn't understand." He sighed. "But if it would help, I could sneak out and ring the doorbell to pick him up."

"I don't know—"

A knife sliced through Ben's chest. "Do you not trust me with him?" If she said yes, it would kill him. He loved that kid and he loved her. If she didn't trust him, there was no hope. They were a package deal. When she didn't answer, he figured he might as well twist the blade further. "We could see if Dale's up and have him take him."

Ben hated that Dale was Cody's father. It was like finding out your father was the leader of the dark side. Not that he knew anything about his father to know what side he supported.

"Ben." Julie rested a hand on his face. "You were a better father to Cody in the time we were together than Dale could ever be. I trust you. I just don't want him to know about us. Yet. It would break his heart if something happened and this is too new." She drew her hand away and he almost whined in protest. "And I feel bad having you Drive-Miss-Daisy my son all over the place."

"What if I want to?"

"Then I would greatly appreciate it." She leaned in and pressed a kiss to his lips. Gentle. Unassuming.

He missed those lips.

She pulled them away too soon. "I need to get dressed."

"You do that. I have to sneak out of the house."

"You do that." She smiled. "Take the side stairs. He rarely uses them."

Julie got out of bed and grabbed her scrubs. A fully-dressed Julie hugging her clothes to her chest. There was nothing sexier.

"I'm really proud of you," he blurted.

"What? Why?"

"You've worked hard, and now you're working in a hospital. That's amazing." He got up and slid his wallet and keys into his pocket. One good thing about not getting naked at night, you're fully dressed in the morning.

Julie's cheeks flamed red. "Thank you." So adorable. He leaned in and kissed her lips. Soft. One kiss for the road.

He pulled away when he heard Cody's laugh. "I should go."

Ben ran a hand through his hair. He probably had the just-woke-up look, but the kid wouldn't recognize that. They could pull this off. He just had to get outside and ring the bell. Easy enough.

CHAPTER SEVEN

EASY. What a joke. Ben stood in the downstairs office listening to Cody giggle.

"Ready or not, here I come, Grandma."

Of course they were playing hide and seek when he needed to sneak by them without being seen. Why wouldn't they be scouring the house at exactly this moment?

A door down the hall whipped open, thunking into the wall. At least he thought it was a door. "Grandma, you in here?" Cody yelled. His voice was like a homing beacon, telling Ben exactly where to avoid.

Feet scampered. And another door swung open. The Byrnes house was big, but the first floor didn't have many doors. And if Ben was correct, the next door to fly open would be to this office.

He peeked at the wide area underneath the desk. He could hide, but since the kid was currently seeking, there was no way Cody wouldn't check under there. Ben surveyed the room. One door. Except...

He hated himself for even considering it. He was an adult trying to be in a relationship with another adult. Climbing out windows was for teenagers—and for people with something to hide. He had nothing to hide. Well. Nothing to hide from other adults, but he did need to hide from Cody. For now.

Ben unlocked the room's single big window and popped out the screen. He'd deal with that later. He got one foot up on the sill so he could angle through the open window and jumped out, closing the window just as Cody whipped open the door. Ben dropped to his knees and ducked, dragging his face through the side of a large evergreen bush till he hit dirt. Thankfully, dry dirt, but it was still dirt.

"Where are you?" Cody huffed and left the room. The office was quiet. The yard was quiet.

Ben stood up, brushing dirt and leaves from the knees of his pants. He was a little worked over, but no one looked good after doing the crawl of shame through the front garden.

"Lost?" Garret asked.

Ben turned, relieved he'd been discovered by a friend. However, the smirk Garret wore made Ben question that. "No. I'm checking how secure the windows on the main floor are."

"Are they secure?"

"Sure." Except for the currently unlocked one in the office with the missing screen. If he told Garret, the man would think Ben was sneaking out like a teen who'd copped a feel. He'd have to tell Julie to lock that before she left.

"Nice clothes. They look like the ones you wore last night." That smirk got deeper and somehow more annoying.

"Why are you still here? Don't you sleep?"

"I could ask you the same thing."

Fine. "It was too late last night to drive home, so I stayed here."

"Me too." Garret laughed. "But they let me use the front door when I left."

"Funny." Ben might have chuckled a bit. It was pretty funny. Well, it would be funny when he was done living through the humiliation. "I don't want to keep you from your rounds."

"You're not keeping me. I thought I'd do another pass before I head home."

"Bye." Ben moved toward the front door, hoping Garret would take the hint.

But the man stood there watching Ben. "Isn't your car that way?" Garret pointed at Ben's Prius.

"Yes, but I need to grab something." A five-year-old, but that counted as something

"Why didn't you grab it before you left?"

"I forgot it."

"Oh." Garret snickered— snickered like a twelve-year-old girl. "Good luck with that, then."

Ben walked up the steps to the front porch and rang the doorbell. He wasn't sure if the bell inside actually rang because the sound was drowned out by the guffaws of an annoying man. With friends like that, Ben needed alcohol. But not until he'd delivered Cody back safe and sound.

"Ben. How lovely to see you." Loraine stepped to the side as Cody barreled into the room and latched onto Ben in a miniature bear hug.

"You're here."

"I'm here." Ben smiled down at Cody's glowing face. "Nice to see you too, buddy."

"I was playing hide-n-seek."

"Did you find her?"

"Yep." Cody rolled his eyes and pointed at Loraine. "She's right there. You're terrible at this game."

"What are you doing here today?" Loraine inspected Ben's clothes up and down. She had to know these were the clothes from last night, but unlike their friend outside, she didn't appear intent on rubbing it in.

"I'm taking Cody to school. Is Julie around?"

"Let me check."

"Julie, honey," she called up the stairs. "You have a gentleman caller down here."

"What's a gentleman caller?" Cody looked at Loraine for the answer.

"A gentleman who calls." Loraine took his hand. "Let's go get your hockey gear."

Cody trotted away next to her. Probably going to the laundry room or some other place where they stored smelly gym equipment. That was where Ben's Aunt Evelyn kept his karate gear when he was a kid. Apparently it was due to little boy smell. Whatever that was.

Julie came down the stairs. Her hair pinned back, wearing a cute set of scrubs. She looked like a nurse. Which was probably the point.

"Thank you so much for taking him today," she said. "Are you sure you can do this? I hate taking you away from work."

"Already texted Allison." He poked at his phone and sent the text. "It's a done deal. I'm taking today off."

"You are a lifesaver. I'll make sure Loraine will be here at four, so you can bring him back here."

"I could take him to dinner so she doesn't have to rush." He wasn't sure what her answer would be. Last night had felt amazing to have her in his arms again, but today was a new day. She might remember she still hated him.

Then she smiled like the idea didn't repulse her. "That would be great, but it's pizza night."

"That's okay. We'll stop for a snack before practice. I haven't had a good guys-only day in a while." He stepped closer to her.

"What's the plan for guys-only day?"

"School. A little hockey." He took another step toward her. He inched into her personal space, waiting to see if she'd stop him. "Maybe some ball scratching."

Her lips curved. She didn't even flinch at what he'd just said. She must not have heard what he'd said. Or she didn't care. To be fair, he didn't care what he was saying right now, either.

"Sounds like an amazing day." Her breathy words jabbed him straight in the gut. His body hummed.

"Should be epic." He moved in closer, and the feel of her breath on his lips slithered down and warmed him in all the best places. He dragged his knuckles over soft skin of her chin, his thumb caressing her bottom lip. Edible. She was fucking delectable. And essential. Essential to his sanity and his happiness. And right now, essential for his next breath.

He leaned in. His lips brushed hers in a simple soft kiss. She opened for him, and the simple became deeper. His tongue tangled with hers. His hands roamed her back. Her groan rumbled in her throat, vibrating against his lips. She was so hot. He pushed his hard body against hers.

She wrapped her hands around his waist and pulled him closer. So close his body pulsed. So close he cursed the clothes separating them. Nothing else existed but her lips. Her body.

"... but I want my green shirt..." Cody's voice cut off. "What are you doing?"

Julie flew backwards, out of their embrace, and Ben didn't have to see his face to know that question was aimed at him... or his mother. Either way, they'd been caught.

"Um..." Julie stared at Cody. "Ben had something in his eye, so I was helping him get rid of it."

Ben couldn't help but smile. She was good. She had lying to her kid nailed down.

"Oh." Cody's face scrunched. "Let me see."

"I don't think Ben has time—"

Cody ran up to Ben and grabbed his hand. "But I want to help."

The thought of a five-year-old's hands poking around his eyes made him cringe. But the kid wanted to help. It was too damn cute.

"You don't have to." Julie wrapped a hand around his arm to stop him from kneeling.

"It's fine." His knee hit the floor, and now his face was aligned with the five-year-old's little hands.

"Be gentle." Julie sighed. Ben could relate. He liked his eyes.

"I will." Cody reached over and ran his fingers along Ben's cheek. His eyes crinkled at the corners as stared at Ben's face. Cody slid his hand gently on Ben's face and pulled his hand away.

He stared at his fingers and then held them out toward Ben. "Make a wish."

"A wish?"

"You make a wish and blow." Cody kept his hand in front of Ben's mouth.

Ben had no idea what was going on. He looked at Julie, and his confusion must have been written on his face.

"You make a wish when you lose an eyelash." She smiled. "You make a wish and blow. Like a candle."

Ben couldn't help the smile that hijacked his face. The kid actually thought Ben had an eyelash in his eye. And he wanted to Ben to blow on it. *This kid.* This kid was his wish. Cody and his mother. That's all he wanted.

He blew on the kid's fingers and Cody's smile bloomed. "Did you make a wish?"

"I did."

"What was it?" Cody inspected his fingers. Ben had a feeling there wasn't an eyelash, nor had there been one. But it was the thought that counted.

"He can't tell you his wish. It won't come true." Julie opened her arms and leaned down. "Now, give me a hug and get going. Ben's going to take you to hockey today."

"Okay." Cody pressed his face into her chest as he wrapped his arms around her.

"Be good." She pulled away. "Thanks," she told Ben as he stood up.

"No problem. I'll have him home by four."

"Perfect. Any time before dinner." Julie smiled. "It's pizza night."

"You should join us." Loraine had a knowing smile on her face. And Ben didn't mind that she knew. Hell, he wanted everyone to know.

"You should." Julie nodded.

The whole thing felt so domestic. He was taking Cody to school and hockey after spending the night with Julie. He was going to eat dinner with them. It felt like family. And he hadn't had family in a long time. "Then I will."

This was dangerous to him. To his heart. But he didn't care. This felt right.

"Ready, squirt?" Ben opened the front door and held the screen door for Cody.

"Don't forget the car seat." Julie pulled one from inside the front closet.

"Got it." He grabbed it, brushing her hand with his fingers. It was all he could do with an audience, but that little touch stained her cheeks red and made him want to kiss her.

"Ready." Cody ran across the porch and right over

to Ben's car.

"Yeah." Ben watched Cody for a second, until the kid got distracted by a bug or something on the ground. Ben stepped into Julie and laid his lips on hers. A quick kiss. A quick promise of later. "Make sure you lock the window in the office." He looked over at Loraine and smiled. "See you tonight."

Walking over to his car, Ben opened the back door and fastened down the child seat. Cody jumped in and wiggled into it. Ben clicked the belt closed.

"Forgot something inside, huh?"

Ben now recognized that voice—and that sarcasm. How had Garret become so annoying? When did that happen? "Yes."

"When you said you forgot something, I thought you meant keys or a hat. Not a kid."

Ben shut the car door and glared at Garret. Of course, a glare didn't shut him up.

"Does Julie know you forgot her kid?"

"Goodbye, Garret."

"Try not to forget him again."

Ben opened the driver's door to the sound of laughter. Closing the damn door didn't drown out the loud hyena sounds.

Dick.

Ben turned the key, hoping the engine noise would drown Garret out. "Ready to start your day, little man?"

"Yeah."

"What?" Ben twisted to face Cody until the belt stopped him. "That didn't sound like you're ready for a super awesome day. They have to hear you on the moon, or they won't take you serious. Are you ready to start your day?"

"Yeah!" Cody bent over and yelled as loud as he could and then flopped back, laughing.

"Then let's go."

———

LATE AFTERNOON, Cody slid out of the back seat and Ben grabbed Cody's hockey bag. The gear smelled so bad, he was afraid to leave it in the car. The smell might never come out. As it was, Ben wasn't sure he'd ever get that smell out of his nostrils.

He had a new respect for his aunt's rules about karate stuff growing up. If it smelled half as bad as the bag in his hand, she should've burned it.

Cody dragged ass walking to the door. Between school and practice, he was worn out. All the yelling and running had been worked out of the kid. They'd done skating drills and played a mock game. Ben had even gotten on the ice after practice and played a bit extra with the kid to wear him out, figuring figured it would help Julie get some sleep tonight. And if she happened to want Ben to hang around and sleep with her, well then that was just a bonus.

Cody opened the front door with a thud. "I'm home." He trudged into the living room and dropped onto the couch. His sweat-soaked hair splayed over the cushion.

"Should you go take a bath before you lay on the furniture?" Ben wasn't sure, but that sounded like a reasonably adult thing to say. If the bag smelled bad, the kid was a walking-talking embodiment of the stench.

"Baths are for babies." Cody huffed but didn't appear to be moving.

He could practically hear the sweat soaking into the fabric. "Then let's get you up for a shower."

"What are you doing here?" Dale walked in the room. Sometimes Ben forgot that Loraine was this guy's mother because Loraine and Adam were such good people. And then there was Dale.

"I'm bringing Cody back from hockey practice."

"Why are you taking my son to hockey?" Dale's voice was angry, his face was angry. What the hell he had to be angry about, Ben had no idea.

"Why are you asking?" Ben lowered his voice, thinking about little ears hearing adult conversations.

"He's my son."

Every part of Ben's body tensed and he literally bit his tongue to keep the words he wanted to say from spilling out. Bad enough the guy left when he found out Cody was his kid. Dale hadn't been back for almost a year. Abandonment didn't even cover it. And Ben couldn't say one word of that in front of Cody, who'd lived it. He didn't need someone putting it into words.

"Boys. Boys. You're home." Loraine came into the living room and glared at Ben and Dale before turning to the sweatball on the couch. "Let's get you in the bath."

"I don't want a bath." Cody's eyes closed. He was beat.

"Then you need a shower. No shower. No pizza."

His eyes popped open. "Pineapple?"

"Pineapple on pizza? That's weird," Dale said, the eye-roll clear in his voice.

Cody didn't say anything, but his face pinched all over, hurt. As far as Ben could see, Dale obviously had no idea his words hurt so much. Then again, Dale was never one to notice what others were thinking. Or maybe he didn't care.

"I love pineapple on pizza." Ben smiled over at Cody. He cared. Cody should never feel bad about liking things others thought were different. They could be weird together. Okay, he'd never had pineapple on pizza. He really hoped he liked it, because he planned on hanging with the kid for a while and didn't want to get caught in a lie. The smile on Cody's face could fuel a power station.

"We'll get double pineapple, then." Loraine reached for Cody's hand and he let her pull him to his feet. "Now, get. Go start the water and I'll be right there."

Cody's shoes scuffed along the floor, across the room and up the stairs.

"Are you sticking around?" Loraine smiled at Ben. So much more welcoming than the glare junior was throwing.

"Sure." It didn't matter what Dale wanted, Ben was here for Cody and Julie and Loraine. All important people in his life.

"I'll be back in few minutes." She spun to face Dale. "Be nice."

"Why are you looking at me? I'm just checking on my son."

"A father doesn't check on his son. A father knows." She shook her head and walked up the stairs, leaving Ben with the father of the year.

"How am I supposed to know anything when the kid won't even let me near him?" The words were a question, but the tone said Dale wasn't interested in an answer.

Too bad Ben was willing to give one. "Cody doesn't know you."

"He knows you?" Dale tsked. "Didn't you and Julie break up? You ran away to play with trees or something."

Wasn't that the tree calling the sapling green. "And you ran away to play with your Russian bride. How's she doing, by the way?"

"I filed for divorce—not that it's any of your business. And Julie and I are working it out."

"Working what out?" Fear trickled down Ben's spine. What did Julie have to work out with him?

"She's the mother of my child and she's been in love with me for twenty years. You don't turn that off."

She had been in love with Dale. Everyone knew it. It probably started in high school. But after Cody was born and she'd started dating Ben, she'd gotten over Dale. She must have. Because if she hadn't, she'd never really loved Ben. And that couldn't be true. His stomach swirled with doubt.

"Cody and Julie are my business." Dale leaned forward. "They are my family. My blood."

"Well, since your son can't be in the same room as you, and Julie can't stand you, I'd say they're not your business anymore. No matter the blood. You don't deserve them."

"And you do?" Dale poked at Ben's shoulder, making him take a step back. "You're just a backstabbing little weasel. It's just a matter of time before Julie finds out all the things you've done. Then what will you do?"

Fury blinded Ben as he drew back a fist. She would never find out. Ever.

CHAPTER EIGHT

JULIE STARED in the rearview at the car tailing her home after her shift. Maybe tailing was too strong a word, but the car had followed hers out of the hospital parking lot and was still behind her. The hospital had been crazy and her clinical had been amazing. She'd had spent all day running around, learning so much about blood draws and vitals. She'd been able to step in and help. It had been invigorating. Plus, she'd worked with a nurse who had over fifteen years' experience. The woman had seen it all and she'd had stories. Julie couldn't wait to have her own stories.

Although finding a guy jerking off when the nurse bent over to adjust the curtains to his liking wasn't one of the stories she wanted to recreate. But beggars can't be choosers.

She was exhausted. And now she was going home to pizza Wednesday. And Ben. She didn't like how much she wanted Ben to still be at the house. Even after so many years of disappointment, especially the past year of disappointment in him—in their relationship or lack thereof.

She turned onto Loraine's street and the car followed closely behind. She stared harder at the rearview mirror, and made out a familiar face smiling from the front seat.

Allison's husband, Adam. Cody's uncle. He was actually tailing her. Ridiculous.

The break-in had happened because someone probably saw the big house and noticed the little one sitting behind it hidden in the trees. Why go after the house that most likely had security when you could go after the little one? Nothing more. It might have had nothing to do with her. So why Allison's husband was trailing her like this was witness protection, she had no idea.

She parked next to Ben's car. He was here. Which meant Cody was home and they'd get to spend the night eating pizza and watching Netflix, together. It was turning out to be the most perfect day.

As she got out of the car, yelling came from the main house. The fact that she could hear it outside told her just how loud they were being. It sounded like Ben, but who could he be yelling at?

Another voice carried out to the drive. Dale. Shit. If they were fighting in front of Cody, she was going to slap them both.

Julie ran to the front door and opened it just in time to see Ben aiming a fist straight at Dale. It didn't look like Cody was anywhere to be found. At least she hoped. She dodged between the two grown men and put up her hands. "What the hell is going on?"

Ben's hand dropped and stepped back. "Nothing."

"Ben was just leaving," Dale snarled.

Julie blinked at Ben. "You were?"

Ben didn't say anything. He just ran a hand down the back of his neck, balling his blond hair in his fist.

"Where's Cody?" Julie asked.

Dale leaned in and gave Julie a hug. "My mom is giving him a bath."

What she would've given for a hug from him a few years ago. Now it did nothing for her. She patted his back and pulled away. "Okay, so why the yelling?"

"Your babysitter is a dick."

"Ben? He's not my babysitter." Not that she wouldn't mind if he wanted to baby sit her anytime. Hmm. That did not sound as sexy in her head as she thought it would. Not that this was the time for sexy, anyway.

"Then what is he?"

The question she didn't want him to ask. She had no idea what they were to each other right now. They were friends who slept together—without the sex. They were ex-lovers who took their kid to hockey. "What Ben and I are is none of your business." Good answer. She pointed at Ben. "And you, what is going on?"

"We were just having a discussion." Ben shrugged. It was the same thing Cody did when he got in trouble. It was kind of cute in an annoying stop-doing-bad-things way.

"About what?" she asked, trying not to grit her teeth.

"About what's best for Cody."

"Is yelling at each other what's best for Cody?" Julie was pretty sure that was a no.

Dale pointed at Ben. "This jerk hanging around my son is not what's best."

Ben glared at Dale. "Having a father who walks in and out of his life isn't healthy. He needs to go—"

"Enough. Neither one of you decides what's best for my son. I have what's best for Cody in my sights. I always have. Always. He is my son." Julie was so close to telling them both to leave, but that wasn't fair to her or Cody. "Ben, you have no right to push Cody's father away. Dale is his father—Cody's family. He has rights."

"You're right." Ben nodded and turned toward the front door. "I should probably go and let you guys do your family thing. I'll see you at work." He disappeared before Julie could tell him to stop.

"We should get ready for dinner." Dale smiled, and she wanted to slap him. Almost. "I bought you some of that ice cream you used to like in high school. I thought we'd have that after dinner."

He bought her ice cream. Why would he buy her anything? "What are you doing?"

He sighed. "What? I just thought we could have a nice family dinner. Why was Mooring here?"

"I had to work, and he offered to take Cody to school and then hockey."

"Why didn't you ask me?" The hurt in Dale's voice was unmistakable.

"You weren't here."

"I couldn't stay in Cody's room all night. My neck started to hurt. I was downstairs, in my old bedroom in the basement."

Julie dropped her school bag and purse on the couch. She'd forgotten she was still carrying them. "I didn't know. And honestly, Cody doesn't even know you to go out with you."

"And whose fault is that?"

"Are you trying to say it's my fault?" Julie's voice rose. After she'd just yelled at Ben for doing the same thing. Fantastic.

"No. But you haven't really included me."

"Included you in what?"

"I didn't know he was in hockey." Dale dropped into a chair. He seemed so tired. Which would have Julie feeling sorry for him, but she'd been on rounds for eight hours for no pay. Her feet hurt. She was exhausted, and the only thing she'd been excited about —dinner with Cody and Ben— was looking more and more like a pipedream.

"Did you ask him? Did you ask me? You've been home for a week and you haven't spent any time alone with Cody. You haven't played a board game or done a puzzle or anything. How is he going to get to know you if you hide away?"

"I just feel like I don't belong." Dale put his elbows on his knees and hung his head. It was pretty pathetic, and Julie wasn't falling for it.

"That's your problem. Grow up and make a space in your son's life for yourself. Or don't. But quit playing this game that you're the one wronged here." Anger pulsed in her temples. She wanted to go lie down, get her blood pressure back to normal human range. But given how the day was shaping up—her heart was going to be beating a heavy-metal rhythm a little bit longer.

———

BEN STORMED out of the house without hitting Dale. That was unfortunate. He didn't want to fight Dale. But all the words coming out of the man's mouth had been true.

Ben didn't deserve Julie or Cody or anyone. He didn't deserve to be part of this family after all the problems he'd caused trying to take over Byrne's and Company. He didn't deserve happiness or anything good.

And she'd made it clear that Dale was back in her life. And Dale made it clear he wanted her. It was only a matter of time before she fell for his bullshit again.

It was better if he walked away now. Made a clean getaway.

"Hey, Ben."

Ben turned to see Adam walking through the trees. Adam was a good guy. And Ben's friend. "How's Julie's house doing?" he asked Adam.

"Good. The room is clean, and the security system will be installed tomorrow morning. She should be back in tomorrow."

"Good." And it was good. Julie didn't need to be

living under the same roof as Dale. At least, not without Ben there.

"What's going on inside? I thought I heard yelling."

"Dale."

Adam spit out a laugh with no humor. "Yeah. He has that effect."

"No offense, I get he's your brother, but how do you deal with him?"

"It helps he's rarely around." Adam laughed, still no humor. "Looking to me for advice on how to get along with my brother is like asking an active alcoholic how to say no to a vodka tonic."

"Did you ever get along?"

"Not for years." Adam shook his head. "He couldn't even be bothered to show up for my wedding."

Ben had noticed that, but hadn't thought about why the guy wasn't there. And the days leading up to the wedding didn't seem like the time to bring down the event by asking. "Did you invite him?"

"Yeah, he was busy."

Too busy to show up at his brother's wedding? Rough.

"Heading out?" Adam asked.

The change of topic was welcome. Ben reached in his pocket for his keys. "Yeah, I'm heading home." Not that he wanted to leave, but he wasn't going to stick around where he wasn't wanted. He'd done that enough through his childhood.

Adam looked over Ben's shoulder. "Julie. Your place is almost ready for you and Cody to move back in." So much for a clean getaway. Ben reluctantly turned around, because it would be rude not to.

"Great." She smiled, but it was forced. Her attention moved to Ben. "Can I talk to you for a minute?"

Adam took a step back. "I'm going to grab my car. Are you going out tonight?"

Julie waved a hand. "No. I'm staying in. Go home."

"I'll see you both later." Adam disappeared between the trees.

"You're leaving?" It was a question, and she might have even sounded a bit upset. But that could be wishful thinking.

"I am." He tipped his head in the direction of the house, where Dale had probably already written her a sonnet to win her back. Dick. "You should go inside to Dale."

"Why?"

"Why what?"

"Why are you leaving?"

"Why aren't you letting me leave?" He was tired and he'd had a really shitty past hour. All the plans he had for how this night would end had gone to hell. He just wanted his own place, with his own bed, and maybe a drink.

"Because you won't talk to me."

"What do you want me to say?" Air flooded out of his lungs. Frustration. Sadness. Maybe a combination of the two. "It would have been great to know that you and the golden boy are trying to work things out. I wouldn't have stayed last night."

"Working what out?"

"Working on being a family again." He didn't have the energy to fight this battle today.

"What does that mean?" Julie frowned at him like he was speaking in tongues.

"I don't know, but according to Dale, you're working on getting back together."

"Me and him." She laughed, a deep laugh that shook her whole body. "Oh, thank you I needed that. That's funny." She swiped at her eyes. "Who told you that?"

"Who do you think?"

Her laughter died. "And you believed him?" She crossed her arms, looking pretty pissed.

He was pissed too. They matched. "Fuck. I don't know what to believe."

"How about you believe me? There is no way Dale and I are working on getting together. In any sense of the word. He needs to work on getting together with his son."

Julie walked over to Ben's car and leaned against the passenger door, resting her head on the roof. After a few deep breaths she said, "We were never even a thing. We slept together once. It's not like we have a deep meaningful relationship we could get back to."

"No. But you share a son." Ben stayed where he was. He had a chance to bolt for the car, and he wasn't taking it. He was a sap.

She raised her head, her body still flat against the car. "We do. But sharing a son doesn't mean we should be together."

"Does he know that?"

"I'm not concerned with what he knows." She turned to Ben and rested a hand on his chest. "I know. And you know." Then she sighed and stepped to the side. "But Dale is Cody's father and he's going to be in Cody's life. And I want you to be in Cody's life. In my life. So I need you to get along with him. For Cody. And for me."

She wasn't playing fair. He didn't want to get along with... What she'd said finally registered. "You want me in your life."

"I thought I'd made it obvious last night and then today." She leaned her body against his. "But if there's any confusion, I really like you. I'm not sure I ever stopped. I want to give us a try."

The warmth of her body seeped into this chest. Her soft parts melding with his hard parts. Like she was the key that fit perfectly inside of him. Which was almost as corny as saying she completed him. But honestly, she did.

"Me too."

"Good." She wrapped her arms around his neck. "Let's do this."

He pulled her closer. His lips ghosted along hers.

"Ben?" Cody's voice came from behind them. Lip-blocked by a child.

Julie dropped her head onto his shoulder. "Raincheck."

"Raincheck." He kissed the tip of her nose and the front door flew open.

"Are you leaving?" The little boy stood on the

porch in feety pajamas. His hair was wet and disappointment was written all over his face.

"I just had to check on my car." Ben walked over to Cody and kneeled down. "Do you want me to stay?"

Cody's face lit up. "Yeah." He grabbed Ben's hand. "I have to show you my homework."

"Homework?" Ben looked at Julie, who shrugged.

Cody dragged Ben through the house and into the kitchen. There, he presented Ben with a picture. A red car with... oblong tires. But the car wasn't what struck him. It was the three people standing to the side of it, holding hands. A man with yellow hair, a woman with short brown hair, and little kid.

"This is great." Ben attempted a smile. "It's your family."

Cody nodded. "That's your car."

"Wow, buddy, that is my car." At least something of Ben was in there somewhere. He'd take it. Ben pointed at the people one by one. "And your mom and dad and you."

"That's not my dad. That's you." Cody lowered his head. "I want you to be my dad."

Ben wrapped an arm around him and closed his eyes. The earth could've opened up and swallowed him fucking whole and Ben wouldn't have cared. This kid. This kid was everything and Ben prayed that he and Julie could make it work, because he was head over heels with both of them.

CHAPTER NINE

THE NEXT MORNING, Julie stood over the sink sucking down a cup of coffee. She'd given up on sitting before work a long time ago. "Cody, let's go."

She turned around and smiled at the kitchen table. The kitchen table where Cody had given Ben his latest art project. A picture of her, Ben and Cody. She'd seen the surprise and adoration written across his face.

She'd fought back a few tears after that exchange. She loved when her boys got along.

Dale shuffled into the kitchen. "Good morning."

"Morning. You're up early."

"I thought I'd see if I could take Cody to school today." Dale had the same tilt of his chin that Cody wore when he was asking forgiveness. "You were right. I need to get involved in his life."

Warmth spread through her body. She'd always wanted Cody to know his father, and here he was. "I'm glad. He'll appreciate that. He needs a father."

"I'm not sure. He was getting pretty chummy with Ben last night."

Grown-man jealousy. Not attractive. "Dale. Ben isn't going away. Can you try to get along with him?"

"Fine. But I don't like it. You don't know everything about him."

"What don't I know?"

Cody's footsteps banged down the hallway and he flew through the door to the kitchen. "I got my bag." As he shoved his stuffed dog into it, a plastic magnifying glass fell out of the bag.

"Why are you taking your magnifying glass to school?" Julie asked him.

"We're playing scientists."

"Who's playing scientists?"

"Me and Toby." Cody slid the magnifying glass in next to his stuffed animal and zipped the bag.

"Okay. Have fun, but do your work. Your dad is going to take you to school today." Julie kneeled in front of Cody and fixed his shirt collar. She turned to Cody's father. "Your mother has a car set in her car. You should probably take her car."

"Okay, Mommy. I love you." Cody looked over her shoulder, and Dale must have done something, because Cody started laughing.

"Should we go?" Dale asked him.

Cody followed Dale out of the back door. As they walked across the lawn and around the house toward Loraine's car, Dale grabbed onto Cody's hand. Cody turned and laughed. His little mouth moving nonstop. Dale smiled down as they walked.

This was what she'd wanted and she could admit it felt amazing to watch them.

"It's nice to see them together like that." Loraine had snuck up behind her. The reverence in her voice matched the feeling in Julie's gut.

"Yeah, it is."

"It's good for a boy to have as many role models as he can."

Julie wasn't quite sure where this was going, but she had an idea. "Ben."

"Yes. You made a good choice giving him another chance." Loraine nodded in the direction Dale and Cody had disappeared. "Both of them."

"I hope so." Both men had a history of breaking her heart. Both men had a history of disappearing. But that had been her whole life. She'd never had a man she could count on until Herb Byrnes, and even he was gone now.

She didn't want Cody to have to live through that—to live through men disappearing from his life like he didn't matter. Like he wasn't good enough. Because dammit, he was good enough.

"I hope so too." Loraine didn't sound like trusting these men with something so precious was a good idea. But the alternative was to close Cody off to other men completely. That wasn't the answer either.

YELLING CAME from Allison's office, and even a closed door didn't stop the noise. Julie slapped her textbook closed. She wasn't going to remember a damn thing about gestational diabetes with that going on, and pretty soon other people would notice. She knocked first, and then opened the door.

Allison leaned over the table, jabbing a finger at the pages laid out between them. Ben sat back and shook his head.

"We're getting noise complaints from Indiana," Julie said.

Allison sighed and dropped into a chair. "Sorry."

"What's going on in here? Can I help?"

"If you can knock some sense into him, yes." Allison waved a hand at Ben, who shook his head.

"I am seeing sense," he said. "We can't pretend to be on the edge of jewelry trends if we don't tell our clients about them. Those bulky bracelets they wanted are out of style."

Allison picked up what looked like a sketch and put it in front of Ben. "Yes, but that's what the customer wants, and the customer is always right."

"That's what he said he wanted. We can give him something that meets his needs but is still fashionable." He picked up another sketch and slid it toward Allison.

"What do you think, Julie?" Allison waved her over.

The pieces in both sketches were pretty. One was a three-band bracelet with large stones. The other was three separate narrow bracelets with fewer stones. The narrower bracelets were cute.

Allison pointed to the sketch with the trio of narrow bracelets. "What do you think of this one?"

That was easy. "I like it. They're simple, but not too

simple. You can choose which bracelet to wear for the day—lots of different combinations."

Ben smiled. "Exactly."

"Fine." Allison indicated the other sketch. "What about this one?"

"Um, it's nice. Colorful." Julie didn't want to get in the middle of an argument between her best friend and her boyfriend. Okay, they hadn't defined it yet. So, friend that was a boy.

"That's what you really think?" Allison was practically scowling.

Julie didn't even blink. "I think I like my job and I like my best friend and I don't want to get in the middle."

"Just tell her," Ben said, mouth quirking. "She already knows."

Allison huffed. "Yeah, just tell me."

Julie exhaled. "I think Bettina has that exact bracelet in her collection."

Allison stared at Julie for a beat before she crumpled up the drawing. "We'll move forward with the trio. Ben, can you run with that? We'll need to present it next week, so the designers should start on it today."

"Of course." Before Ben left the room, he winked at Julie.

Heat crawled up Julie's neck as she turned to follow him out.

"So, what was that about?" Allison asked before she could escape.

"What was what about?" Julie would like to think

she was playing dumb, but she really had no clue what Allison was talking about.

"That look you gave Ben."

Oh, that. "What look? I didn't give him anything." Now she was playing.

"Really? One day he's talking about taking you out on a date—a date which was preempted by the break-in —and now you're making googly eyes and winking."

"I didn't wink." *She* didn't.

"Oh, I know. That was your little boyfriend out there."

"He's not my boyfriend."

"Are you sure?"

Julie threw up her hands. "I don't know. We haven't defined it yet."

"So there's something to define."

A knock sounded from the open door. Ben stood there with a smirk on his face. "I called down to the designers. They're working on it now."

"Great," Allison said.

The telltale sound of "Single Ladies" came from Julie's desk. Her cellphone. Probably a fake call. Either her long-lost cousin the sheik needed her to wire money, or the IRS had suspended her social security number. That didn't stop her from dashing out to her desk and grabbing the phone.

Cody's school. Crap. She had class tonight. If Cody was sick—which was the only reason his school ever called—she'd never make it to class.

Much as she hated missing class, she'd just have to send in the assignment. Maybe jumpstart on the next chapter. She took a breath and made peace with the idea of an evening with a little man and Pedialyte. "Hi. This is Julie Connolly."

"Ms. Connolly, I'm calling from Cody's school." The woman's tone was clipped. Usually, when the nurse called her voice was sunshine and lollipops. "You didn't call to inform us that your son would be out today."

"Because he's not out today. He's there."

"Well, Ms. Pool marked him absent."

"It must be a mistake. He's not absent. His father dropped him off this morning." She'd watched Cody and Dale walk out the door. Cody could be persuasive —maybe he talked Dale into grabbing something to eat on the way to school. Unless the teacher just missed him.

"I'll head down to the classroom." The woman's tone gentled.

"What's going on?" Ben asked, flanked by Allison.

Julie covered the phone. "Allison, call Dale. Find out where he is."

Allison disappeared into her office, reappearing with her phone to her ear. She mouthed "Voicemail."

This was all a mistake. Phone still glued to her ear, Julie pulled out her purse and searched for her keys. It wasn't like she'd need to leave. Cody would be sitting in his desk, and all this would be something they'd all laugh about one day. Not today. But one day.

Muffled voices came across the line, and a familiar woman's voice spoke in Julie's ear. "Hi, Ms. Connolly, this is Ms. Pool. Cody's not here today. One of the teachers thought she saw him earlier with a man, but he's not here now."

Dale. They saw him with Dale.

Julie's knees gave way, and thankfully her chair was behind her or she would have hit the floor. Not that she cared. "Who saw him? When was this?"

"I can get the teacher, but we should really call the police and you should come down here."

"Yes, of course." Julie stared at her keys. It was over an hour drive to the school. An hour of not knowing.

"We'll see you soon. I'm going to call the police."

"Yes." Julie ended the call. Her mind was still trying to catch up to what was happening. That's the only excuse she had for why she wasn't running out of the office at this very moment.

"Julie, what's going on?" Someone said the words. Julie couldn't be sure who. She had to get to Cody.

"Did you get a hold of Dale?" Julie asked Allison, amazed at how calm she sounded. "He walked Cody to school today. But Cody's not there."

Allison shook her head, phone pressed to her ear. "He's not answering."

"I need to get there. The administration is going to call the police." She picked up her purse. "I need to be there."

"You do." Ben rested a hand on hers. "But you shouldn't drive. Let me drive, and you can focus on getting hold of Dale."

What he said made sense. She'd never be able to concentrate on driving. "Okay."

"Help her find Dale," Allison said into her phone

and then clicked off. She was pretending to be calm. But she sucked at it. "I'm sure Dale just took him to get something to eat or something. He's so irresponsible. I called Adam. He's going to call his mom and search for Dale and Cody."

Julie nodded, throat too tight for words, and she and Ben walked toward the elevator.

"I'll stay here, just in case Dale shows up." Allison followed them over to the elevator, and as the door opened, she added, "Ben, please keep me posted."

He nodded, and hit the button for the lobby once Julie stepped inside. As the doors slowly closed, he said, "It's going to be all right. It's Dale being Dale."

Julie tried to smile and nod but couldn't manage both. She prayed it was Dale being Dale. Yes, she'd be pissed. But as long as Cody was safe, she could handle it. As long as he was safe, she could handle anything.

And if he wasn't—if her baby wasn't safe—there weren't words. She couldn't even think that way. She'd never be able to handle anything again.

▭

BEN STOOD in the principal's office. Chaos. Cops.

"The only reason I noticed him was because he was so cute," the teacher was saying. "And I'd never seen him before. It's not like I notice all the men, but I notice parents."

It had been two hours, and they were still no closer to finding the kid than they were before. They hadn't found Dale, either. Adam and Loraine were scouring the city. They'd checked coffee shops, ice cream shops and any other shop where there was an abundance of sugar.

So far, nothing.

"So, you saw this man bring Cody to the school," the cop said. "Did they go inside the building?"

"I don't know." The teacher shook her head. "They both came into the playground, and Cody was showing him how he could use the slide. Then Declan and Craig started fighting, so I went to break them up. By the time I was done, it was time to start class."

The police officer nodded. "Thank you for your time."

The teacher exited, leaving two officers, the principal, Julie and Ben. The silence was loud. Everyone avoided the elephant suffocating the room. Cody was gone, and it wasn't a mistake or a misunderstanding.

Ben couldn't take it any longer. "So what do we do now?"

"Now we investigate," the one cop said. "You both need to go home and see if Cody or his father show up at the house."

"I'm just supposed to sit there and do nothing?" Julie's glare could melt steel.

"Yes." The officer stood. "I'm sorry. I know this is hard, but let us handle this. We have a lot of resources. More than likely, Mr. Byrnes took your son to Great America or something. Especially given everything you've told us about him. Go home and wait for them to show up with cotton candy and floppy hats."

Ben almost believed it. Or maybe he just wanted to

believe it. He took Julie's hand. Her fingers were ice cold. Somehow, she looked smaller. More fragile.

"Let's go back to the house." He wrapped an arm around her shoulders and she leaned into him. As they made their way out of the office, little kids, Cody's age, ran down the halls screaming and laughing.

Julie's shoulders stiffened under his arm. Her breath hitched and he didn't have to look to know that she had tears in her eyes. His eyes were steaming up, too. Knowing that Cody should be here laughing with all of these other kids—and knowing he wasn't.

They somehow made it through all the adorable children and outside to the car. He clicked the locks, opened the door, and Julie slid in the passenger side. She didn't say a word. There wasn't anything to say.

Anything they could say would drown them in sorrow. If they didn't talk about it, there was still hope. And right now, hope was the only thing making it possible for him to start the engine. The only thing helping him drive to Loraine's. The only thing preventing him from breaking down.

He needed to be strong for Julie, but the thought of never seeing that kid about killed him.

CHAPTER TEN

IT HAD BEEN TEN HOURS. Ten hours since she'd last seen her son. Ten hours since he'd said "I love you" in his little voice. His arms had wrapped around her waist.

Every minute he wasn't found was a knife to her heart. Every minute she didn't know where he was killed her. Was Cody being treated well? Was he scared? What did they want?

Whatever it was, she'd gladly give it. If they wanted her arm, her leg, her heart, her life... anything. Just call. Send in the order. She'd hand over everything she owned to get him back.

They'd set up everything in Loraine's living room. Julie's phone had been hooked up to some sort of tracker machine, and they were waiting for a ransom demand. No one had called, so all the fancy recording equipment sat dormant. Silent.

The rest of the room buzzed with activity. Julie just

stared at her phone, willing it to ring. Maybe with Dale on the other line telling her he took Cody to the arcade, or the mall—or something.

"They weren't at the zoo," Allison said, checking another location off the whiteboard they'd listed possible places on. Ben was on the road with everyone they knew. Combing stores and parks and monuments. And here Julie sat. Doing nothing.

Okay. Maybe not nothing. She'd kept herself busy playing the part of good hostess. She'd made room for the electronic equipment and tables. She'd put together sandwiches and coffee for all the cops who'd walked through the house. Most were out searching the neighborhood, which was great. But that meant she was running out of people to serve. And when she wasn't serving, she was staring and thinking. Neither made for strong mental health.

"Can I get you more coffee or another snack?" she asked the man fiddling with the recording equipment.

"No thanks. I can't eat another bite, and if I drink anymore caffeine, I won't be able to sleep tonight." He patted his stomach.

She didn't have the heart to tell him she wouldn't sleep tonight, no matter what. "Okay." She tried to smile. That's how Loraine did it—service with a smile. Julie didn't want to act like everything was all right. She wasn't all right. Her smile was inches away from seceding from her face. And she didn't blame it.

She wanted to secede from her life.

"Did you find Dale?" Allison pulled the phone away from her ear as the person on the other end got louder and louder. "So that's a no." Allison brought the phone back to her ear as a small smile found her face and parked on her lips. "Just be careful and keep calm. We'll find them both."

With a click, Allison's phone hit the table next to the whiteboard. She added an X next to the children's museum. "They haven't found Dale, but Adam's heading back here. He wants to start covering the neighborhood with fliers."

"Does Adam think Dale took Cody?" The thought shouldn't have been swimming around her head, but she couldn't stop it. Dale was back for a few days, offered to take Cody to school, and now they were both missing. Too many coincidences.

"I think he does." Allison tossed the marker onto the table. "But I don't know. What would Dale gain from taking him?"

"Maybe he's just took him someplace fun." Was that what grasping at straws meant?

"Maybe, but don't you think he would have called or come home by now?"

The last shred of hope shriveled up in Julie's chest. Allison was right. Dale wouldn't just disappear with Cody for this long and not try to reach out. He would try to call or he'd just come home. Unless there was something wrong. "Maybe his phone died." Her voice squeaked.

His phone had to have died. It was all she had left before she delved too far into what *something wrong* really meant.

Allison nodded, but she didn't look convinced. "I'm

sure his phone just died and he took Cody to some pool hall or something and lost track of time. You know how he gets."

Five-year-old Cody in a pool hall didn't exactly keep the worry at bay. She could just see some gnarly biker starting a fight with the soft and squishy Dale. And her son getting caught in the crosshairs.

"Stop!"

Julie turned to Allison, wondering what she wanted stopped, but Allison was looking at Julie. Who wasn't doing anything.

Allison said, "Wherever your mind is going, make it stop. Cody will be fine. We'll find Dale, and all of this will be something you laugh about when he's graduating high school. Okay, maybe college."

"I don't think I'll ever laugh about this."

Allison crossed the room and wrapped her arms around Julie. "I know, sweetie. I'm sorry."

"Ms. Connolly." A familiar man came into the living room. Probably one of the many nameless, faceless people wandering through the house. "I'm Detective Barrows. I want to show you something. Do you have a DVD player?"

"I have one," the tech behind the phone equipment said, and produced a laptop.

"Sorry it took so long to get this footage," the detective explained, "but the security company had certain protocols to follow. This is when Cody comes into view with your ex-husband."

"He wasn't my husband," Julie said automatically.

Barrows nodded and started the video. "Cody and his father. There's no sound."

The screen filled with a grainy picture of the front of Cody's school. Children ran and played. Swings swung. Totters teetered. Teachers stood talking to parents and watching the kids—until they didn't. The female teachers all turned left as Cody and Dale entered into view. One woman blatantly checked Dale out, up and down. He was a nice-looking guy, which was probably why it took Julie years to get over him. But she had.

Cody ran toward the slide before stopping. He turned to Dale and said something with enough anima-tion for those cartoons he loved, and then jumped into the line for the slide. As Cody climbed up the ladder he yelled over to Dale—probably to make sure he was watching. Cody always did that. Like they could miss him. He sat at the top of the slide and wiggled his butt. It gave him better flying power. At least that's what Cody told her when Julie asked why he did that. Reaching forward, Cody tugged himself into move-ment, sliding down and landing with both feet planted on the ground. He raised his arms over his head like an Olympian after a dismount.

Dale clapped and gave his son a high-five. Was this when Dale decided to take Cody? Maybe bond more with his son? Was this the point when Dale felt he deserved quality time—to hell with his son's education and Julie's worry?

Dale leaned down to Cody's level and said a few

words. Cody launched himself at Dale. A sweet hug with his father. Even with the shoddy picture and the small screen, Cody's smile came through. The kid had been in heaven with his father back—was. He was in heaven with his father back. He was happy, not in heaven. Julie couldn't think about heaven right now. Not with Cody missing.

How many times had she wanted this for her son? How many times had she held him because his father wasn't there over the past year? Too many to count. Yet, there they were.

Dale pulled away as the teachers waved their hands and pointed to the front door of the school. Teachers ushered the kids inside, and parents walked out of view of the camera, most likely to their cars.

Cody ran to the slide. He could never pass up a no-line opportunity. He slid down with minimal theatrics, and stared off to the left—where Dale had just disappeared. He just stared. Her mind filled in everything the grainy recording was missing. His rounded cheeks. His blue eyes. She wanted to reach out and touch the soft skin of his face. She wanted to tell him, wherever he was, it was all okay. She wanted to scream. She wanted to vomit.

She wanted him back.

Tears built in her eyes and she knuckled them away. This was her only link—her last link to her son. She didn't have time to cry. She needed to watch him. The way he tilted his head when he was concentrating. The way he kicked his foot when he wasn't sure what to do.

He stared off to the side as students ran to the front door and teachers broke up a fight on the other side of the playground. He continued to watch as more students ran into view when parents dropped them off at the last minute.

Cody twisted right, toward the school door, and then back to the left. Watching...what?

Go to school. Turn around. Whatever you're watching, don't follow. She knew he hadn't gone into the school. If he had, they wouldn't be here right now. But nothing could stop her from thinking the words and praying the whole thing would end differently.

Make good choices.

Don't leave me.

A smile widened his mouth, visible even with the crappy picture quality, and he ran left. The whole video clip probably only took minutes, but it felt like days. Students still poured into the school. Teachers still separated fighting students. No one noticed Cody walk away—out of camera range.

No one saw him disappear.

The video stopped and the monitor went black— like the sadness that lodged in her throat.

Detective Barrows stopped the disc and took it out of the laptop. "I'm sorry you had to watch that, but we wanted to talk about the video."

"Sure." She could barely find her voice.

"Could he have gone after his father?"

"Of course." Cody would probably do anything for one iota of attention from him. "His father was new to his life, so he would do anything."

"New?" Barrows looked up.

"Dale just moved back to the States a little over a week ago."

"Where was he?"

"With his now-ex-wife somewhere. I don't know. Russia, I think." She shook her head, because she really didn't know, and she didn't care right now. All she cared about was her son.

"Could he have taken Cody back with him?"

"Like hell." The voice wasn't hers—but they were her words. The voice was Ben's. She turned around, and Ben and Adam hovered in the doorway. They must have come in at some point. She didn't know when. Specifics and situational awareness weren't her strong suit today.

"We'll send out an Amber Alert and send something to the airports and trains." Barrows slid the CD in his pocket. "Since this is a parental kidnapping situation, at least you know he's with someone who wouldn't hurt him."

Little consolation. But she was pretty sure Dale wouldn't hurt their son. "Can I have that?"

Barrows didn't flinch, but something in his demeanor said the words before he said them. "I don't think that's a good idea."

"Why?"

Allison laid a hand on her shoulder. "I'm sure the police need the video as evidence."

"Didn't you make a copy?" Julie hoped the tears starting in her eyes would get him to listen. "I need that disc."

Barrows sighed, and finally handed her the CD. She wrapped both hands around the plastic case and held it to her chest. This one connection was all she had until she got him back. Something to let her see him. She'd made videos when he was younger, but as he got older things always seemed to get in the way.

This was her son. Today.

Allison reached for the disc. "Let's put this away before you crack it."

Julie nodded as she let go of her lifeline.

Barrows handed Julie a card. "I should go. But notify me if you think of anything that might help. No matter how small." He walked out the front door. And then there was silence.

Well, mostly silence. The computer guy talked to Adam. Allison talked to Ben. And Julie ignored it all. She had to be missing something. Dale wouldn't do this. He wasn't cruel.

He was reckless and irresponsible, but he wasn't dangerous. Why would he take Cody and just vanish? The answer was that he wouldn't. Which scared her more than anything, because that meant that someone else had her son.

BEN STOOD IN THE DOORWAY, trying to keep his anger bubbling under the surface. Not letting it out. Not letting Julie see it. She stared at the floor as if it kicked her puppy. Right now, he felt like he'd been kicked. He could only imagine how she felt.

That video. He'd watched the tail end, as Cody watched Dale. That look of pure adoration on his little face. The kid wanted his dad. Bad enough to run after him. Bad enough to miss school. Probably. That didn't explain why Dale had taken Cody.

It didn't explain anything.

"Why don't you take a shower?" Allison suggested to Julie. "I'll come get you if we hear anything."

Julie's eyes closed—like she wanted to think of a reason not to go. But in the end, her eyes opened and she nodded before she left the room. No fight. No argument. As if she was beaten.

That killed him.

"She's not herself." Allison sighed. "I don't know what to do."

"There's nothing we can do." Adam put an arm around her shoulders. "All we can do is what we've been doing. Helping with the search. Being here when she needs us. An APB went out an hour ago. Hopefully, we'll get a hit soon."

"But what if we don't?" Allison's eyes filled with tears and a hiccup stuttered out of her throat.

Adam squeezed her shoulder. "We can't think like that."

"I know, but he's just a kid. He shouldn't be out there on his own. Or worse..."

Ben couldn't even begin to think like that or he'd spiral into a blubbering mess and they didn't have time for that. Not now. Not when there was still hope that they'd find him.

"I just can't sit still. We need to be out there look-ing." Allison dropped her face into her hands, tears rolling down and pooling at her chin.

"We have people out there," Adam said into her hair. "The best thing for us to do is man the phones. If we leave, Julie will be here alone."

Ben left the room. Not because all the touchy-feely was making him uncomfortable—although it was. Not because he hated watching Allison cry—although he did. He walked away because Allison was falling apart and had Adam to pick up the pieces. This was Julie's son, and who was there for her? Ben. That's who. And no matter what Adam said, she wasn't alone. Never.

Standing in the living room wasn't doing any good. He made his way upstairs and listened at the door of the room where she was staying. No sound. No swish of water. No sounds of Julie in the room. He knocked on the door.

Nothing.

"Julie, it's Ben." He knocked again, and then tried the knob. Locked. He sighed—praying she'd open the door and he wouldn't have to kick the thing open. It looked easy in movies, but he had a feeling that the solid oak doors would take a kick from The Rock and not just someone—himself, for example—who worked out on a semi-regular basis.

Ben knocked on the door, again. "Julie?" Worry rose in his throat. Yes, he was panicked. But she wasn't opening the door. There was no sound from inside the room. Where the hell would she have gone?

He jiggled the handle. Still locked. He took two steps back and cracked his neck. This was either going to be a gallant gesture or an epic fail. Either way, he prayed it didn't end up with him in traction in the hospital.

He drew his left foot back. A little running start never hurt anyone. Well, it might hurt, but he was trying not to think about that.

The door flew open. Julie stood there. So pale. Her clothes the same as when she'd left. No anger. No fear. Nothing.

"Were you taking a shower?" Ben asked.

"No." She turned away and dropped onto the bed.

"What are you doing?"

Julie stared straight up. "Waiting."

The mattress dipped when he sat next to her and laid down. She rolled sideways, resting her head on his shoulder.

He had to admit it was nice to have her this close. Maybe not the circumstance that had her leaning on him. He hated that Cody was missing. But he was glad she was taking the only thing Ben had to offer her. Comfort. He ran a hand along her back. Soft strokes that burrowed her head deeper into his shoulder. "They'll tell you if anything comes in," he said softly.

"I know." Her eyes drooped closed. She needed rest. It had been a long, emotional day. And until they heard something, there wasn't a reason for her to fight sleep.

"Why don't we lay down and take a nap?"

Her eyes flew open and she struggled to sit. "No! I can't sleep."

"Okay. No sleep. Let's get you some tea."

"With caffeine." Her eyes already started to droop before he got off the bed.

Despite that, he headed for the kitchen. By the time he got back, hopefully she'd be passed out.

JULIE WOKE TO YELLING. At least she thought she was awake. The room was dark, and she was on the bed. Someone was next to her. Ben.

More yelling form downstairs. The light on the clock said 2AM. Who would be awake?

Ben angled up. "What was that?"

"I don't know." Julie sat up, her head spinning like a bad hangover. She hadn't gotten drunk last night, not with her and Cody staying at Loraine's.

More yelling.

Wait. Cody was missing.

"Cody." She scrambled out of bed and whipped open the door. Ben was right behind her.

"Where the hell is he?" That was Adam. Yelling.

"I took him to school." Dale's voice arrowed up the stairs and stabbed Julie in the throat. Dale was here.

"Where the fuck did you take him?" Adam demanded.

Julie flew down the stairs and was on top of Dale

before her feet hit the hardwood. Her body slammed against him, knocking the wind from her chest. But that didn't matter. Nothing mattered except Cody. She grabbed Dale's collar and shook. Shook. Shook him. Hoping that one of the shakes would produce her son.

Dale looked stricken. He looked like she felt. He couldn't have taken him.

The air in her lungs thinned. Everything—the house, Dale, Adam, Allison, Ben— around her disappeared. Cody was gone and someone took him. She didn't know where to even begin. A black hole slowly enveloped her.

No! She didn't have time for this. Self-pity. Wallowing. Those weren't on her agenda. They couldn't be.

Ben pressed up behind her. His chest molded against her back. "Are you okay?" he whispered in her ear.

"I'm fine." Julie leaned against Ben and closed her eyes. She soaked up his warmth—his strength. She could do this. She would do this. "Adam, should we call the police? This isn't a parental kidnapping any longer. We should get the detective back here to reevaluate."

"I'll send him a message." Adam pulled out his phone, already in cop mode. Five seconds ago, he was in Dale's face, yelling. Now, nothing.

"Dale, tell me what happened." Julie controlled her voice, but barely. He was the last one to see her son.

"I told Adam—"

"Tell me." The look in her eyes must have told Dale she was not playing. She might not be able to shake the information out of him, but she'd gladly beat it out of him.

Dale sighed. "I watched Cody on the slide and then the teachers started yelling for the kids to come inside. I told him to go, and watched him walk toward the door. Then I left."

"You didn't wait for him to go inside?" She knew the answer. Why did she even bother asking the question?

"There were teachers around, and other kids. I didn't think to watch him." Dale's already pale face turned an interesting shade of white. "I'm sorry. I didn't know to watch him till he got inside. I didn't think—"

"No. You didn't think," Ben snarled. "Why would you think about your son when you could—what—go out drinking? Drugs? I can smell the booze from here."

Julie turned in his arms and laid a hand on his chest. She had to get Ben calmed down. They all had to be calm. "It was his first time taking Cody to school. He couldn't have known."

Ben's eyes lasered on Dale.

"Look at me." Julie cupped Ben's cheek. "It doesn't help if we're on opposite sides. I don't know how many times I've left him outside to play before school. I never would have thought this could happen."

Ben looked at her, all the pain in her chest written clearly on his face. The man was hurting and it broke her heart, but the only thing she could do about it was find Cody.

Without breaking eye contact with Ben, Julie asked, "Adam, what do we do now?"

"We make some coffee." He tapped at his phone. "The detectives are coming over now."

"Now?"

Adam gave her a small smile. "It's good to know someone in law enforcement to push things along."

"Thank you."

Adam nodded. "Allison, let's go make some coffee."

"Anyone want anything else?" Allison asked.

Dale shook his head and stumbled over to the couch.

"Coffee's fine." Julie leaned into Ben and buried her head against his chest.

"I'm sorry." The words brushed along her hair, his breath warm on the top of her head.

"For what?" She tried to pull away but Ben's arms tightened. She swore she felt tears hitting the top of her head.

Ben shook his head, rocking his cheek against her hair. "I'm losing my shit, yelling at Dale. You have enough problems, you don't need me making things harder."

She tried to pull away and he held tight. Not this time. She angled her head back and pushed until his arms fell to his sides. "You don't make this harder. You make it so I can function. I don't mind you yelling at Dale. Honestly, I wanted to do it myself. But it would have just caused problems and we need all hands on deck."

Speaking of which... She reached for his hands and put them on her hips before moving in close and wiping a tear from the side of his eye. "You said the things I shouldn't. And I'm thankful for that."

"I just want to be there for you."

"You are in so many ways."

"Are you sure?" Ben gently pulled her to him.

"I'd tell you if I wasn't."

"You would, wouldn't you." His eyes were no longer sad, but assessing. "There was a time you wouldn't have told me. You wouldn't have pushed me away or put me in my place."

That was true. There was a time she would have just endured so she could have had him in her life. "I'm different now. Is that bad?" Not that she cared. She didn't think it was bad, but she didn't want to be with someone who didn't see all the changes she'd made as positive.

"Not at all." He drew her close. "In fact, I kind of like it."

"Good, 'cause this is me."

"Well, I like *me*."

"I like me, too." She smiled into his T-shirt.

The doorbell rang. Moment over. Reality sucked back into the room with one set of beeps. Probably the cops. Probably here to figure out what was next. Hopefully what was next was finding Cody.

Julie didn't know how long she could keep this up. Every second her baby was away was killing her.

TWENTY MINUTES LATER, Ben listened to the cops ask Dale question after question. Dale answered as expected. And, unexpectedly, Ben hadn't yelled at the idiot once. Not that he didn't want to.

Dale swore that he wasn't in any trouble—this time. That he didn't need money and no one was coming after him. Ben believed him about as much as he believed in the tooth fairy.

"So, Ms. Connolly, since this is no longer a case of parental abduction, we've brought in the FBI. Special Agent Laramie has some questions."

When Barrows mentioned her name, Laramie set her tablet next to her on the couch and folded her hands. "I understand you've spoken with Detective Barrows and I've seen the report. I apologize if there is overlap, but any information you can share with me, even if it feels ridiculous or disconnected to the case, I need to know."

Something about Laramie was calming, and Ben found himself nodding along with Julie.

Laramie went on. "We need to broaden our search. We need to investigate the people in your life and in your son's life." She leaned forward and picked up the mug of coffee Allison had put in front of her earlier. "Is there anyone who holds a grudge against you?"

"Me?" Julie shook her head and took a sip of her own coffee.

Everyone at the office loved her and Cody. They were like family. What Ben didn't know was her life outside of work. "No one from school?" he suggested.

Julie glanced off to the side, thinking, before she shook her head again. "Not anyone I can think of."

"You aren't in competition with anyone?" Laramie asked.

"Nothing like that. I have a full-time job and a child, I'm barely getting by." Julie's voice hooked on the word *child*. Although Ben saw a crack forming in her composure, she merely cleared her throat and continued. "No one is going to be jealous of my academics."

Laramie nodded. "Have you started going anywhere new?"

"Nothing new. I've been going to my gym for the past year. And even that, I haven't been there in over a month. The gym is more of an in-between-semesters thing."

"What about Cody?" Laramie set her coffee down, waving off Allison's silent offer of a refill.

"Cody hasn't started anything new either. He's been in the same hockey club for two years." Julie's gaze clouded before her eyes sparked. "But there was something weird. When I went to pick him up the other day, the coach mentioned that someone was sitting with Cody and talking."

"About what?"

"She asked questions about me. Did I pick him up from school every day or did I work?"

"Did he answer?" Agent Laramie picked up her tablet.

Allison edged closer and topped off the mug in Julie's hand. Julie nodded and Allison smiled. She was fraying at the edges, too. They all were.

Julie lowered her mug, and looked away from Laramie and Barrows. "Yes. Cody told her that I picked him up, but not all the time because I work in Chicago." It almost seemed to hurt her to answer.

"Was this after the break-in?" Barrows shook his head, reproach clear in his grimace.

"No, not after. Before." Julie's shoulders slumped. "I didn't know."

"You didn't know what?" The FBI agent's voice was soothing.

"Nothing." A tear slid down Julie's cheek.

"What didn't you know?" Laramie asked again.

"I didn't know that someone talking to my son could lead to this. I swear."

The FBI agent nodded. "Of course not. Who would think that? Well, at least this gives us a starting point. We'll want to talk to the coach and anyone else who was there that day."

Julie nodded as the agent woke her tablet and typed into the screen. "One more thing, and I know this sounds weird. But we have to cover all the bases. Does anyone have anything against Cody? A disgruntled teacher, or angry parent."

"Is that even a thing?" Julie asked the question Ben had a feeling they all wanted to ask. What kind of sick person would hold a grudge against a five-year-old?

Laramie's mouth tightened. "Unfortunately, it can be."

"I don't even know how to answer that. He's five. My son doesn't have enemies. He has playdates."

"I understand. But could anyone hold anything against him or your family?"

Julie looked around the room, maybe looking for the answer. But given the blank looks, no one was going to pass this pop quiz. "I yelled at his preschool teacher last year. Miss Carter still won't talk to me, but I wouldn't think she'd hold a grudge."

"We'll look into her." Laramie tapped at the screen some more. "We haven't received a ransom demand, but I wouldn't be surprised if we hear from them shortly. Any unusual people come into your life recently? Repairmen. New mailman. Anything."

"Loraine had some work done in the back yard."

"I'll get you their card." Adam stepped away from the wall and headed for the kitchen.

"Anyone else?"

"No. There hasn't been anything unusual."

Ben couldn't imagine a time when things had been less normal. "Well, if you don't count the break-in, the weird hockey interrogation and that her father passed away."

"True." Julie's brittle smile hurt Ben's chest.

"Your father passed. When?" Laramie asked.

"A week ago."

"Anything unusual about the funeral or the death?"

"No. He died of natural causes."

The agent stood up. "Thank you all for your time."

"Thank you for coming out this early," Julie said as Adam walked back in the room.

"This is the contractor my mother used for the back yard." Adam gave Laramie the card and followed her to the front door. "I can't thank you enough for coming out. I know it's early, but once we realized Cody wasn't with Dale, I wanted to get a jump on the next leg of the investigation."

"Understandable." Laramie slipped the card into her bag. "If it was my nephew, I'd be pushing hard to find him, too. If you remember anything else or if you hear anything, reach out."

"We will." Ben put his arm around Julie. She slid out from under it and headed toward the stairs. As the cops left and Adam closed the front door with a click, Ben headed after her.

She might try to run, but Ben wasn't going to let her hide.

CHAPTER TWELVE

JULIE WAS SO TIRED. She'd been woken up by screaming a couple hours ago. The sun still was barely up. Everyone was doing things but her. They were out searching, they were manning phones, and all Julie did was wait. She was so tired of waiting—and they were barely through the first day. What if it went on longer…?

No. She couldn't think that way. She couldn't think about Cody being out there alone. Never knowing…

Allison's sister Brook, her boyfriend Joe, and a group of others had been searching all day and night. And they hadn't stopped.

"Is there anything I can do?" Julie asked Adam. "Maybe I should go out with Brook and Joe to start looking?"

Adam ran a hand through his hair. He looked exhausted. "They're working in shifts. The night shift is combing the streets and parks and anywhere else they think he might be."

"Maybe you should take a break," Julie suggested.

"You should too. Those couple hours of sleep aren't enough."

Julie started to protest and Adam stopped her. "I'm not trying to be a dick here, but you're no good to anyone exhausted. Try to get some sleep. In a few hours, we'll get up and start all over again."

All over again. But what if tomorrow was as bad as today? Her face must have given her thoughts away, because Adam moved closer and put his hand on her arm.

"Hey. We'll find him. You have the FBI and the support of the Chicago PD. We're not giving up and neither should you."

A tear slid down her cheek as she nodded. Julie leaned into Adam and gave him a hug. "Thank you so much."

"We're family. There's no thanks in family."

Another set of arms wrapped around from behind Julie, and long blonde hair slid along her shoulder. Allison. Julie admitted, "I don't think I could handle this without you all here."

"We're here. We're not going anywhere." Allison pressed Julie against Adam. A Julie sandwich, minus the pesky breathing.

"Ummm..." Julie spit out between gasps of air.

"Sorry." Allison let her go. "Shay should be here soon. She's going to cover the phones so I can take a nap. Wake me up if you hear anything."

"I will," Julie promised.

"Julie, you should go to bed too. Shay or the cops might need you during the day."

She nodded. She had to go to bed. She had to trust that they'd keep it all under control down here. She made her way upstairs, and someone grabbed her arm.

Ben.

She tried to smile. She wanted him with her tonight and she'd forgotten to ask him to come up. But he knew. He always knew. She turned to the one person she could not get through this without.

The someone holding her arm wasn't Ben. It was Dale.

"Are you okay?" Dale asked.

She didn't bother answering the question.

"Yeah. I guess not." He slid his hands into the front pockets of his jeans. "I just wanted to say I'm sorry. I've spent so little time with him and I don't even know what to feel. You have been his everything for so long and everything with your dad—I just— I'm sorry. I know it doesn't mean much, but I'm sorry for everything."

"It's okay, Dale. Go to bed. We'll figure everything out in the morning."

Dale's face fell and his eyes crinkled in guilt. "I won't be here."

Julie felt the anger bubble in her chest. Dale was leaving. Again. When her son—his son needed him. The anger flowed through her body, steeling her spine. Her fists clenched. She wasn't really a fighter, but right now felt like a good time to start. "You're leaving?"

"There's a search crew leaving at four AM. I'm

heading out with them. I'd head out now, but Adam said I should sleep first. They need me sober." Dale's head dipped. "I was out drinking when our son was being..." Dale's eyes glistened as he lifted his head. "I have to find him. I'm sorry."

"You didn't do anything wrong. Nobody knew this would happen."

"But I should have been here. I shouldn't have been out drinking when our son needed me." Dale was voicing all the things that Julie felt. She might not have been drinking, but she'd been at work going about her day. How many time had she wanted to just put Cody in a plastic bubble and protect him from bullies or pain. How many times had she wanted to drop everything for that kid?

But she knew she had to give him room to grow—room to have his own life. And this was the cost.

Dammit. Why did it have to be so hard?

"I should get to bed." Dale ran his hand over his eyes, wicking away the moisture. He pulled her in for a hug and she hugged him back. Dale might be an idiot but he'd given her the best thing in her life—Cody. "I'll see you tomorrow when I get back."

"Sure." Once inside her bedroom, Julie closed the door and leaned her head against it. She didn't want to be alone tonight. She didn't know how fair it was to want Ben here. They hadn't even defined anything yet. But that didn't stop her from pulling out her cell phone and sending the text.

She pulled out a pair of pajamas and waited. No response. He might have headed home. The guy was probably exhausted. She couldn't expect him to stop his life because hers was falling apart.

The door rattled as someone knocked. She whipped it open to find Ben in the hall.

Thank God.

He walked in and wrapped his arms around her. "I wasn't sure if you'd want me to stay," he whispered into her hair, like he was revealing a long-lost secret.

His body was strong and solid, and her insides melted as she soaked up all his strength. "I wasn't sure if you'd want to stay."

"Where else would I go?" His arms tightened, but she pulled back a bit to look into his eyes.

"I don't want you to feel like you have to stay. I know you have a life and this is not your problem."

His arms disappeared, his face drawn in pain. "You're not my problem? Cody's not my problem?"

"I don't mean it like that."

"What do you mean it like?"

"We haven't defined what this is. Hell, we haven't even gone on a real date." Her voice rose. This wasn't what he wanted to hear, but it needed to be said. She wasn't looking for emotional handouts. "We barely spoke for the past couple years and now that we're talking, this happens. I don't know what we are. And I just feel like I'm dragging you into my drama."

"I've been clear for the past year what I want." Ben crossed his arms over his chest.

This wasn't coming out right. "I don't want you to feel obligated."

"Obligated to care about you and Cody?"

"No. I know you care about us." She shook her head. "It's more an obligation to comfort me like you have been. I needed you, and you've been there."

"Of course, I've been there. Whatever happens between us, we're friends. Friends comfort."

"Is that all we are?"

"It's not all I want to be, but we don't have to define it right now." He leaned in and rested his chin on her head. His hands stayed at his side. "All I know is I want to be here. You think you need me? I am barely holding on. You're all I have."

She nodded. "You're all I have, too."

"Let's gets some sleep."

She pulled away from him and his arms, knowing she'd climb back in once she was in bed. Hell, that was the only reason she was able to pull away at all. She slid under the covers of the large bed and guilt wrapped around her throat. She'd just gone five minutes without thinking about Cody. Five minutes with her mind on something else.

Those five minutes slammed her with enough guilt to stop a freight train. It weighed on her chest. It strangled her heart.

She needed to get Cody back. She couldn't live like this. She didn't want to.

———

JULIE SCRUBBED THE STOVE. Not that it wasn't clean, but it gave her hands something to do. It gave her something to think about other than the nightmares that had plagued her. And every time she'd woken up she'd cried herself to sleep again and again—quietly enough to make sure not to worry Ben.

Cody locked in a closet. Cody being beaten, violated. His little body enduring torture. Death.

She scrubbed harder. The muscles in her arm screamed. Why wasn't this stove shiny enough yet? All the what-ifs were killing her. All the scenarios breaking her heart and cracking her spirit down the center. A seismic shift that would never be fully healed and only grow deeper the longer Cody remained missing.

"Any news, sweetheart?" Loraine came into the kitchen and poured herself a cup of coffee.

"Nothing yet." Julie turned her rag loose on the island as Loraine started a fresh pot of coffee.

"I think it's clean," Loraine told her, stopping Julie's pruney hand mid-swipe, and gave her a kind smile.

"I know, but I need to do something."

"You could get dressed." Loraine tipped her head toward Julie.

Pajama pants, T-shirt, and Snoopy slippers weren't inappropriate morning kitchen wear, but Julie could admit they were a little midlife crisis. Cody had given her the slippers, though, and she needed a piece of him near her right now. And getting dressed in real clothes before the sun had risen hadn't been on her radar. "I will." Later.

"I could make you something to eat," Loraine offered.

"I'm not really hungry."

Loraine dragged the rag out of Julie's hand and

shook her head. Smiling, she drew Julie toward the kitchen table. "Have a seat. You have to eat something." She opened the big box of pastries on the counter and took out a cruller. "Eat this and I'll get you some coffee."

Julie stared at the donut. Just stared. She'd spent a year exercising and eating healthy to lose weight. Because if she'd lost the weight, she'd be happy. And she had been. But it hadn't stopped the pain from losing Ben. And it didn't stop the pain from not knowing where her son was.

And here she was thinking about putting carbs in her body. A slippery slope for someone with a food addiction. But part of her didn't care. What was the point of denying herself when everything could go to shit at any second? What was the point of taking care of herself?

Cody.

Cody was the reason for most of what she did. The day he was born, her life had shifted. She'd gone from being the center of her world to protecting the center of her world. And he was the center. Without him she was hollow. Her heart was gone.

So was the point of eating healthy.

She grabbed the donut on the table and took a bite. The sugar should've melted on her tongue. The light flaky twists should have been delicious, but somehow it was like sawdust.

"Have some coffee." Loraine put a cup on the table before sitting down beside Julie.

"Aren't you covering the phones?"

"I am, but I wanted to make sure you're okay first."

"I'm fine. Go to the phones. Then Brook can start searching."

Loraine stared at Julie for a second. It was disconcerting being watched like a caged monkey. "Okay, dear." She stood up and left the kitchen.

Not five minutes later Ben walked in. "You're eating a donut. When was the last time you had carbs?"

And he'd paid attention. How sweet.

"Since we were in Vegas." She'd spent the past year dreaming about bread while eating vegetables. Except for the group's vacation to Vegas. Granted, that was more work trip than vacation. There had been a lot of carbs—mostly in liquid form. She'd been trying to drink Ben away.

"Do you want me to make you some eggs? You want some fruit?"

"Eggs would be great." Julie got up and moved the plate with the cruller to the counter. It wasn't worth the calories if she wasn't going to enjoy it. "Want a donut?"

Ben smiled and grabbed a bite of donut before disappearing into the fridge. A carton of eggs appeared in his hand. "Cheese?" he asked from the depths of the Sub-Zero.

"Yes." Always yes to cheese. She was on a diet, not dead. And she was also not sitting here waiting. Again. She was so sick of waiting.

"You still like scrambled?"

"Yep." She smiled. She shouldn't be surprised he remembered everything. But somehow, she found herself more and more impressed with him.

More sizzling as the eggs hit the pan.

"Um, Julie?" Ben set two plates of food on the table. "Time to eat. Why don't you eat first, clean second?"

Julie stared at the rag in her hand. She set the rag and the spray bottle of cleanser on the counter and backed away like they were set to explode. How bad was it that she didn't remember picking them up? Julie washed her hands and sat down at the table.

She grabbed a fork and took a bite of the eggs. Not the same as a donut, but she also didn't feel like she was going into sugar shock.

"I'm heading out to search the forest preserve behind the high school. You should come with." Ben sat in the chair next to hers.

"But what about staying here?"

"Do you really want to stay here?" Ben asked around a bite of eggs. "You have a temporary cell phone, and it doesn't hurt to get out for a little bit."

The idea of doing something—anything besides scrubbing furniture—gave her heart a tug. Her cell phone was currently in the living room attached to some device tracker, so she was using a temporary phone. Her friends had the number. And she was finally going to be helping.

"Ms. Connolly." Special Agent Laramie walked into the room carrying a large cup of coffee. On one hand, Julie was glad to see her, on the other, she wasn't sure she wanted to know what Laramie had to say.

"Good morning, Special Agent."

Laramie nodded and rested a hand on a vacant chair. "May I?"

"Sure." Julie hoped that wasn't one of the chairs she'd just sprayed, but Laramie sat down and didn't complain.

"We went through your house, to see if the perp left anything behind. We noticed there were shoe prints going up to Cody's window. And his window was unlocked."

"He sometimes unlocks it so Spiderman can get in if he's in the neighborhood." Julie wanted to cry. Why hadn't she checked the window?

Laramie pulled out a photo. The inside windowsill was missing a chunk of wood. "The police didn't focus on Cody's room at first, since they thought the intruder was after you, however, the intruder might have come in his bedroom first, and when he wasn't there, gone to yours."

"We would have noticed this." Julie would like to think they would have noticed a hunk of missing wood.

"It's not noticeable when the window is shut." The FBI agent leaned back in the chair. "Between this and the stranger in the gym, we think Cody was the target all along."

All along. He was the target. A lump fossilized in the back of her throat, making it hard to breathe. "Why?" Julie's voice wavered. Her whole body shook.

Ben reached out and folded her hand in his. She wanted to pull away, but she needed him right now. She needed someone to hold her hand and tell her it was all right.

But it wasn't all right. And she sure didn't deserve his comfort. She'd let this happen. It was all her fault.

"That's the question." Laramie sipped her coffee. "We're still working on motive."

Ben asked, "Could it have something to do with her father's passing? Maybe someone thought there was an inheritance?" He wound his fingers through hers like he was afraid she'd let go. He knew her pretty well, but her wanting to let go had nothing to do with him asking questions about her father. Ben glanced at her and added, "What about your father's will and the two hundred and fifty thousand?"

Laramie stopped mid sip. "What two hundred and fifty thousand?"

Julie took a breath. "My father offered me money to give custody of Cody to his girlfriend."

Laramie's fingers flew over her tablet. "When did this happen?"

"A few days ago. But my dad couldn't actually kidnap my son from the grave." Although if anyone could, it would be him.

Honestly, she wouldn't be surprised if her father was somehow involved. But with the whole dying thing, he didn't have the means or opportunity.

"We'll look into the girlfriend. Anyone else know about the money?" Laramie's eyes were glued to the screen in her hand.

"There wasn't that much money," Julie said. "He'd lost most of it before he died."

Ben shrugged. "I know that and you know that, but could someone have been confused?"

"Maybe a coworker or someone in your class." Even Laramie was getting in on this.

Julie shook her head. "But wouldn't they have asked for money?"

"Yes, but maybe they're waiting to scare you," Ben said. "The longer you wait, the more you'll be willing to pay."

"But I have nothing to pay with."

"This is just a theory." Ben squeezed her hand, and said to Laramie, "I don't think anyone at Byrnes and Company would take Cody. They know Julie has no money."

"But his grandma has money," Laramie said, nodding to indicate the high-end kitchen.

"Everyone knows that." Julie disengaged her hand from Ben's. There was obviously money here. But the people at Byrnes and Company were her friends.

"Maybe someone was in dire need," Laramie said. "Could someone be in a position right now that they might benefit from extra cash?"

"Everyone." Julie crossed the room to move her attention out the window. Anywhere but here answering these questions—worrying about her son. If she twisted her head just right she could see the corner of her little house, just beyond the back yard. The little house where she was raising her son. Pain stabbed at her chest.

God, she missed him.

"...Marinda in payroll's husband has cancer and had to quit work. They are barely making ends meet. Donny's wife just gave birth to triplets."

Julie tuned in to what Ben was saying. "Those aren't reasons for kidnapping. Those are our friends and their problems."

"One man's problem is another man's desperation." Agent Laramie had her tablet out and was stabbing at it like it cheated on her—probably everything Ben was saying.

"Everyone has problems," Julie snapped. "Tabitha's husband is cheating and if he leaves her, she can't afford to live on her own." This was a needle in a haystack. She needed Cody back now and opening up the list of suspects wasn't going to make it happen any quicker. "Brice has a gambling problem. Rick drinks too much. Anyone and everyone could be desperate enough."

"Which is why we question them all," Laramie said, the picture of patience.

Julie hated this. Hated worrying that her friends might have done something so heinous. Hated that she would even entertain the idea. "What do we do now?"

"You relax and wait by the phone."

She hated relaxing and waiting by the phone, too.

Laramie nodded and left the kitchen. Silence. Julie didn't know what to say. Instead, she sifted through the pictures Laramie had left on the table.

They'd all thought the perp entered through Julie's sliding glass door, since that was how they'd left. Why hadn't she looked closer? Why hadn't she questioned everything? Why hadn't she walked Cody to school—kept her eyes on him every second of every day? Especially after a woman approached him, and then the break-in. For heaven's sake, what did she need, flares?

How could she have been so stupid?

"Are you okay?" Ben finally spoke, but Julie didn't have the heart to answer. She picked up her plate, half-filled with food, and dumped it in the garbage. Then she walked over to the sink and turned on the faucet. She scrubbed the plate with a sponge. Rinsed it. Scrubbed it again.

Ben cleared his throat. "Talk to me."

"I'm fine." She turned the heat up on the water until steam billowed from the sink.

"You're not fine."

Of course she wasn't fine. "What do you want from me? I'm doing the best that I can." And even that wasn't good enough. She set the clean plate in the dishrack and started on the fork, running the sponge over the tines again and again.

"Julie." Ben's voice was right at her ear, and the sympathy grated on her nerves. She didn't need sympathy. "I'm worried about you."

"Don't worry about me." She threw the fork onto the rack. "There's nothing to worry about with me." She was fine, absolutely fine. There was nothing wrong with her. "Worry about Cody. He's the one who's out there. He's alone and afraid." And it was all her fault. A tear poked at the back of her eyes, but didn't fall. She'd cried so much over the past day, she didn't have anything left. She sniffled. She was empty. "I'm here and I'm fine."

"Can't I worry about you both?" He reached out his

hand and touched her arm, but she pulled away. She didn't have the energy to lift her chin. She knew it was Ben and she loved him for caring, but she didn't deserve it.

"I need to be alone." She couldn't take the pity or the pain she knew was building. He tried to pretend he was strong through all of this, but he was falling apart, just like she was.

"Do you want me to leave?" The pain in his voice was clear. So was the guilt. He thought he was doing something wrong.

She closed her eyes and breathed deep. "I'm ruining everything."

"Ruining what?"

"This is all my fault." She wanted to cry. There was no way for the sadness in her chest to get out. "I should have known what was happening. Someone tried to break into my house, and started asking Cody questions."

"You couldn't have known—"

"I didn't have to know. I had to act." People broke into her house and strangers approached her son. And she did nothing. Nothing. What the hell was wrong with her? "What the hell did I need to happen to take things seriously? Skywriting? Maybe a personal invitation to keep a closer eye on my son."

"It's not your fault." He just didn't get it. And he never would. And it didn't matter. None of this mattered. All that mattered was getting her son back. Once she knew he was safe, she'd make a choice. The hard choice. She'd do what was best for him.

She hated to admit it, but her father had been right. She should've listened. She was a terrible mother who didn't deserve Cody. She couldn't even handle his basic safety, let alone the needs of someone so gifted. This was God's way of reminding her of that.

CHAPTER THIRTEEN

BEN HAD no idea what to say. This was all his fault as well, so he couldn't judge. But he hated seeing her this way. "This isn't your fault."

He knew it meant nothing. He could say it until his last breath and she wouldn't believe it. He wouldn't believe it either, if someone said to him. But it didn't stop him from saying it. He reached for her hand and she didn't pull away. Progress.

Julie squeezed his hand and straightened up. "It doesn't matter. I need to find him." She took out two to-go cups and filled them with coffee. "There's another group going out in a few minutes. I'm going with."

Ben looked her up and down and didn't say a word. He didn't have to. Julie looked at her Snoopy-covered feet and sighed. "I can't go out like this. Can you tell Brook to wait for me?"

"Go get dressed. We won't leave without you." Ben leaned in and kissed her forehead. He watched her walk out of the kitchen, a new fire in her eyes. He missed that fire. And he was so thankful it was there.

He walked into the living room, the hub of the action, although there wasn't much action right now.

Brook handed Loraine a card. "When a call comes in on Julie's phone, we just answer. The machine automatically records the call, and the tracer tracks the location. If anything comes in that's strange, call the officer."

"Do you think I should be the only one here?" Loraine looked at the phone like it might jump up and bite her.

"There's no way to mess it up." Brook patted her on the back. "Just answer it if it rings."

"How often does it ring?"

"It doesn't." Brook shook her head. "Most of her friends already called, and they don't want to tie up the line."

The cell phone on the desk rang. Brook stared at it. She had the same look of terror as Loraine. And neither one picked up the phone.

Ben answered the call. "Hello."

"This is Special Agent Laramie, is Julie there?"

Ben held the phone away from his mouth and whispered to Brook, "Go get Julie." She looked at him with wide eyes and ran out of the room.

"Did you find him?" Ben asked.

"I need to talk to Julie first."

"Is he okay?"

Laramie didn't say anything. Not. One. Thing.

Scenarios ran through Ben's mind, but he shook his head before any of them stuck.

"I'm here." Julie ran into the living room, T-shirt hanging down over bare knees. Ben handed her the phone and waited.

"This is Julie." Silence. She nodded, but her expression didn't change. Ben wanted to shake her when she said, "Mm-hmm." Another silence. She clicked end before she turned and bolted.

"Well?" Ben yelled at her back.

"Sorry." Julie paused, one hand on the newel post. "They think they found him, but I need to go now."

"Where?"

Julie yelled words that were probably English, but he wouldn't testify to that in court. Less than a minute later, she ran back down the stairs, this time in pants and shoes, too. "Let's go." Her car keys jingled as she headed straight for the front door. Ben followed behind. To help. To find out what the hell was going on. Both, really.

She ran for the car. Brook trailed Ben. "Where are we going?" Brook asked.

"They think they found him." Julie slid behind the wheel and started the car.

Ben dove into the passenger seat at the same time Brook jumped into the back. Before their doors clicked shut, the car lurched backward.

"A new student started at a school in Joliet, and the assistant principal called the police." Julie sounded grim. Or maybe that was because she was backing up at high speed.

"Why? Don't new kids start all the time?" Ben fumbled with his seatbelt while the car sped down the road. Loud pings sounded as pebbles pelted the side of the car.

"Yeah." Julie took a right, heading toward the southwestern suburb of Joliet. "But they don't normally get a new student that has an Amber Alert photo."

Excitement bubbled in Ben's chest. He'd heard of Amber Alerts. He knew they existed, but he'd never thought about how they work. And if this principal saw a picture of Cody, the kid had to be Cody.

"The vice principal saw Cody's picture." Julie's eyes sparkled. "And he recognized him. I cannot even…" She bounced her hand on the steering wheel as she drove.

Ben tried to tamp his excitement down. He didn't want to feel it. Not until he had Cody in his arms. But as they made their way to the tollway, Julie's excitement was contagious. And it felt really damn good to feel something other than fear.

━━

JULIE STOOD near the window in the principal's office—a place she never visited when she was a kid. She was the good-girl daughter of a high-powered lawyer. Her father would have never accepted her getting in trouble.

The red brick building was quiet inside. The kids were in class. And Cody was in there somewhere. Her hands tapped the side of her leg. So close yet so far. She wanted to sit still but, again, he was so close.

Outside, children played, ran, and screamed in the playground. None of them Cody. She'd looked. She'd had the time.

Ben walked up next to her and slid his warm hand into hers. Her hammering heart slowed in her chest. Just his touch calmed her nerves. Her fingers stopped tapping. They could get through this. Together. Getting through this sooner rather than later would be preferable.

She sighed. "What's taking so long?"

He squeezed her hand.

"They're probably waiting for Agent Laramie." Brook sat in the chair in front of the desk. She was a lawyer. She knew what she was talking about. On the other hand, why did they need the FBI here? All they needed was her to bring her son home.

Or at least they could let her see her son and then wait for the police to verify that he should leave with her. But making her wait was just torture. And totally unnecessary.

The door to the office opened and the principal walked in. Thank goodness. Julie watched the door and waited for Cody to come up behind her. But no one came.

The principal closed the door. Instead of the bright smile she'd worn when they'd first walked in, the woman was frowning. She stood by the door, a mixture of guilt and sadness written across her face. "First of all,

I'm so sorry for the wait. I wanted to thank you for coming here today, but our assistant principal jumped the gun. We contacted the parents of the new child."

Julie heard the words the principal was saying, she just couldn't seem to understand what they meant. "What?"

The principal opened the office door. "I'm sorry."

A little boy with blond hair walked in. Cody's height. Cody's hair color. But definitely not Cody. "This is Samuel. He started here today."

Julie had no words. This was the boy. This was the boy that could be her son. But wasn't. Her son wasn't found.

"Hi, Samuel." Ben kneeled in front of the child, his smile as brittle as Julie felt. "It's nice to meet you."

"Hi." The little boy waved and looked around the room. He looked confused and scared.

Like Cody. Who wasn't here.

"Samuel, follow the assistant principal back to class." The principal smiled warmly at the boy. She closed the door and walked behind her desk. But she didn't sit down. She stood there with her hands crossed in front of her. "I'm so sorry for the confusion. Samuel's parents dropped him off but didn't come into the office. My assistant principal saw a resemblance and called the police. Once I found out what was happening, I pulled the boy from class and phoned his emergency contacts. We were able to get in touch with them a few minutes ago."

"Cody isn't here?" Julie knew the answer. The

woman had been explaining all of this in great detail. But until Julie heard the words, there was still this small kernel that held out hope. That somehow her son was here. That this was a kismet-type event that didn't sidetrack them from finding Cody but was an accidental lead.

"I'm so sorry, but, no. Your son is not here. We did not find Cody, it was Samuel."

Julie nodded as tears bit the back of her eyes. Despite all the crying she'd been doing, those tears were finding a way.

"Oh, I'm so sorry. Please don't cry." The principal held out a box of tissues.

"You're sorry?" Julie's mouth formed the words, but it wasn't she who said it. Brook stood from her chair. "Is this some sort of joke? You've played with the emotions of a scared family and you tell her not to cry. What kind of monster are you?"

"I didn't mean—"

"What did you mean when you told her not to cry?" Brook's eyes were red and she looked on the verge of tears herself.

"Brook." Julie squeezed her friend's arm.

"What?" Brook's tone changed as the anger in her eyes dimmed. "Sorry. I just..."

"It's okay." Julie didn't think any of it was okay. But it wasn't Brook's fault. In fact, she was trying to help. "We should go."

"I really am sorry," the principal repeated.

Julie just nodded and walked out the door. What

was there to say? Everyone was sorry, but there wasn't anything anyone could do. They were trying to find a needle in haystack. With every day that passed, that haystack was getting larger and larger.

CHAPTER FOURTEEN

JULIE COULDN'T HEAD HOME. She could not face the house again. She needed to move. She needed to forget. She tried not to think about the school as they drove to the site of the search party. She could never understand why anyone called it a party. It didn't feel like a party. Nothing about today felt like a party.

"We're here." Ben parked Julie's car in the Campton Forest Preserve parking lot. On the other side, Joe stood in the center of a group of people.

"I'm going to go see when they're leaving." Brook jumped out of the back seat and shut the door. Running up to her boyfriend, she wrapped her arms around his neck. Joe caught her and held on. They both looked tired.

So did Ben. "Are you all right?"

"I'm fine." Julie didn't want to think about how far away she was from fine. And talking about it would only make her dwell on it. "I just want to get out there."

Moving around and looking for her son would help her feel better. At least she hoped it would.

"Then let's go." Ben took her keys from the ignition and tossed them to her.

Julie stepped out into the chilled air. It was spring, but summer still hadn't shown its face. She walked over just as one of the searchers stepped into view. She wore a black pea coat and light pink scarf, and her perfect blonde hair was held in place with a light pink head-band. She looked just like her mother, without the evil glint in her eye.

"I heard you might be coming out today." Bettina's daughter Emily patted Julie's arm. "Are you okay?"

Julie was so tired of that question. She considered writing *I'm fine* on a piece of paper so she could hold it up every time someone asked. "I'm hanging in there."

"You are." Emily nodded. "This must be so hard. I can't even imagine."

Julie nodded. What was she supposed to say to that?

"My mom is so worried about you."

Yeah right.

Emily must have missed the you-have-to-be-shitting-me look on Julie's face because she kept talking. "In fact, she's worried about all of us. She thinks this all has to do with your father's death. She's hired security for each grandchild and increased security at the house."

"Really?"

"She's totally paranoid. She bought steel doors and replaced all the windows with reinforced windows."

Reinforced windows would have come in handy with the break-in. One more thing in a long list that Julie should have done to ensure Cody's safety.

"Luckily, my children go to a private school with security, so we don't have to worry about sending the security guards with them..." Emily's face paled.

She must have heard that Cody was taken from his school. The school that was so inadequate that her son was snatched right outside it. The school that wasn't challenging him or giving him what he needed because of Julie's selfish need to keep him close to her.

"I'm so sorry. I didn't mean anything by that. I'm just nervous. I don't know what to say." Emily's mother might be awful, but Emily had always been nice. Now, her sister Heidi was a nightmare, but she wasn't here. Thank goodness.

"Don't worry about it." Julie smiled.

"All right everyone. We're going to have four teams." Joe spoke up from in front of a police cruiser with a map laid open on the hood. "Team one—" He pointed to himself, and then pointed at each volunteer in turn as he called out numbers. He finished up with, "Ben and Julie, team four." He waved everyone over to stand over the map. "Team one is following this path, leading to the back of the preserve. Teams two and three will split off and follow these side paths. Team four will enter on the preserve on the left side and follow the inner loop."

Julie had been here before and knew the inner loop was shorter. They'd be done in no time. And the rest of the teams would still be working. "What do we do when we're done?"

"If you finish early, there are connector trails here and here." Joe pointed to the top of the loop. "Take one of the trails until we all meet up here. Each team will take a walkie."

Julie nodded and selected one of the walkie-talkies from a box on the roof of the car. Brook handed her a flashlight, saying, "It gets dark under the trees. This could help."

"Thanks." Julie clicked the flashlight on and off to make sure the thing was working. She was determined to find Cody, no matter what.

The other groups had combed the town where they lived. But he could have wandered off and got lost in the forest. And if that had happened, she'd find him.

The group collected gear and discussed the plan, but Julie didn't have time. She knew her route. She knew she had to go. The afternoon breeze carried a bite of cool, but the sunlight warmed her as she walked across the parking lot to the path entrance on the left side.

Trees rustled and leaves swirled with every gust of air. The path called to her. She had to look. She had to find him. At the edge, the trees formed a canopy of darkness. Inside, oaks and evergreens towered over-head, blocking out any splattering of light.

She turned on the flashlight and sent its beam into the shadowed crevices of the bushes and trees lining the path. Without the warmth of the sun, the forest was dead cold. Sloppy leaves covered the path. The scent of pine and dirt coated the air. The temperature dropped further as she walked, but Julie didn't care.

"Julie, slow down."

She stopped, pointing the flashlight at the path behind her. Ben jogged up, carrying a map. "I thought we might need this."

"Thanks." She appreciated the map, but she needed to keep moving. She was finally helping, and wasn't about to sit still.

"I grabbed another flashlight, too."

Julie nodded started walking again.

Ben caught up to her, leaves crinkling, and the glow from his flashlight bobbed up and down. "Why don't you take the right, I'll take the left?"

"Okay." She trained her light on the righthand side of the path. No movement. Nothing.

The radio crackled at her hip. "First connector trail, clear." Oops. She hadn't stuck around long enough to know when she was supposed to call in. She was sucking at this.

"Are you okay?" Ben asked.

"Fine." Julie paused when she caught movement off to her side. Just a swaying branch. Probably from the wind.

"Fine? You're quiet."

She knew he was looking at her because his voice grew a tad louder. And she knew he was worried. But there was nothing to worry about. "I just want to find Cody."

"We all do." He sighed and touched her arm. "But I want you to know you can talk to me."

"About what?" She pulled away and kept moving. She didn't want to talk. It was overrated.

"About how you're feeling."

She definitely did not want to talk about that. She snorted a laugh with no humor. "You really want to talk about your feelings?" Guys never wanted to talk about their feelings—especially if you called them out on it. At least that was the plan.

"No. I want you to talk about your feelings."

She stopped and turned to him. "That doesn't sound fair. I have to talk about my feelings but you don't." She unclipped the radio as they reached the end of the trail. "Second connector trail, clear." That seemed like the right way to do it.

"I feel powerless." Ben's voice was far away. Like he wasn't walking with her anymore.

Julie stopped. Turned around.

Ben faced her from several feet away. "I feel angry and scared. And I hate that there isn't one fucking thing I can do about it. I hate watching you try to hide what you're going through. And I hate myself for not doing more, pushing harder when the break-in happened. I should have said something. Done something. But I was mad about Dale. About him being here. And I let this happen." Ben shook his head and aimed the flashlight at the left side. "That's how I feel."

Julie moved close enough to twine her fingers through his. He didn't look directly at her, but he didn't need to. She could tell he was crying, and given how wavy the world was looking, she was crying too.

"I'm sorry." He ran the back of his arm over his

eyes. "I'm supposed to be strong for you. Not the other way around."

"You don't have to be strong. Just be you." Julie closed her eyes and let the sounds of the forest envelope her. The crinkle of blowing leaves. The whir of the wind. "I feel all of that and more."

"What's the more?"

She didn't want to get into the more. He wouldn't understand.

"Julie, talk to me."

"All of what you said. It's not on you. It's on me. I hate myself for letting this happen. I hate that there's nothing I can do. I hate that my father was right. I don't deserve him."

"You can't believe that."

"Why can't I? I can't even keep him safe."

"Julie—"

"What? He was right. And him being right doesn't even bother me. He's been arrogantly correct my whole life. He has proven me wrong time and time again. So it doesn't matter. But this time. This time I wanted him to be wrong. This time I wanted to show him…" Despondent laughter bubbled in her chest. "I wanted to show a dead man that I deserved Cody. That Cody would be better off with me. But he's not. And it kills me."

Her tears blurred everything around her and there was nothing she could do to stop them. She'd just admitted the one thing that plagued her every day since she got her father's letter.

"What are you saying?"

Julie wiped her eyes and swung her flashlight to the

right side of the trail. "I'm saying nothing." She couldn't even say it out loud. When they found Cody, she was going to talk to Bettina.

If it killed her.

▭

BEN WALKED with Julie back to the car as the teams disbanded. Joe and Brook collected gear and waited for the last of the searchers to return. No one had found anything. Which was good and bad. Even so, Julie wasn't talking. He'd tried to get her to say something— anything— but she was lost somewhere in her head.

Something was wrong. He couldn't quite put his finger on it, but the way Julie talked about Cody and her father told him something was going on with her. And not just the fact that Cody was missing. Something was off.

"Why don't we grab something to eat before we head home." He pulled out his keys.

"I'm not going home."

"It's been a long day—"

"If you want to go home? Go." Julie's fists slammed against her hips. "I'll ride with Brook and Joe."

"I don't want to, but I think you need your rest."

"Why?"

He didn't want to answer the question. It felt like a trap. No matter what he said it would be spun to make him out to be a grade-A ass. So, he needed to come up with a nice way to say you look like crap and you're acting weird. "You seem—off." There, that wasn't so bad.

Her nostrils flared, and her face took on a lethal red hue. Lethal for him, not her. "What does that even mean?"

Nope. Not going there. He liked living.

"My son is missing. Don't you get it?"

Pain that felt close to betrayal snapped at his chest. "I get it. Don't you think I know? But you're saying things about your father. Things that aren't true. And you're scaring me."

"Well, my son being missing is scaring me. I can't think. I can't breathe. I can't go back to that house and stare at the walls. I can't." Julie sighed and waved at Brook. "I'm coming with you."

Julie sighed and tugged her jacket closed. Like suddenly she was cold. Even though the disappearing afternoon sun was shining. "Go home, Ben. Get some rest."

He watched her walk away. Just disappear into Joe's car. She didn't wave or even look his way as the car's tires crunched over the gravel and leaves. The car disappeared from view. She disappeared from view.

He didn't know what to do anymore. No matter what he said or did, it was wrong. It's like nothing he did helped. But he got it, he understood. This was hard for her, but dammit, this was hard for him too. He loved that kid. Like Cody was his own.

Like. That little word made all the difference. He could always love the kid like his own, and he would lay his life down for him. He could adore him and care for him and be the best man he could—all for Cody.

But Cody wasn't his. Cody was hers. She'd carried him for nine months and loved him and sacrificed. She'd never ran away from him. Fuck.

He didn't understand. He could never understand. And here he went pushing her away when she needed him the most. Part of him wanted to chase after her. Explain that he got it now—he'd never understand. But the other part knew she needed a little space. And he'd give her anything she needed right now. Because even though he might not understand, he knew she was in pain and he refused to cause her more.

He spun her keys on his finger, and got in her car. He was starving. He'd grab something to eat and then drop off the car. He'd give her the space she needed.

TWO HOURS and a bucket of chicken later, Ben pulled in alongside all the other cars lining Loraine's driveway. Between the security staff, cops wandering in and out, and the search party members coming and going, the house seemed constantly in motion.

Ben walked around to the back of the house, which was quieter—except for Adam standing in the center of the yard, phone glued to his ear.

Anger morphed Adam's face from the normally stoic to the downright scary. Whatever the caller was saying on the other end wasn't making the guy happy. In fact, Ben had never seen the guy this angry.

"Why the fuck aren't you vetting these Amber alert

calls?" Adam snapped, and then was quiet for a moment. "I get it, but I'm not sending Cody's mother on these bullshit calls... Call me, not her."

He slammed his finger into the phone and sighed. "Dammit." His head hung low as he ran a hand through his hair. The guy was losing it.

"What happened?" Ben had been out of the loop for two hours. He wasn't gone days. How did something happen in that little time?

Adam sighed again. "Julie got another call that they'd found Cody."

Son of a... "And I'm guessing from your tone, they didn't."

"No. Another false report." Adam shoved his phone into his back pocket. "Julie doesn't need this. She broke down and cried. Joe called while Brook tried to console her."

"I don't know how much longer she can hold on," Ben admitted.

"We need to find Cody."

"We're doing everything we can though, right?"

"Yeah." Adam huffed a huge breath. "It just feels inadequate. I think I'm heading in to talk to Agent Laramie. There has to be something we're missing."

"Good idea. Keep me posted if there's anything I can do." Ben held up Julie's car keys. "Can you make sure Julie gets these?"

"Where are you going?"

"Home."

"You're leaving her? Now?"

"She wanted me to leave. That's why I'm not with her now."

"She's distraught. She doesn't know what she wants." Adam sighed. Again. And he didn't look like he was feeling any better. No matter how many times his lungs deflated. "Don't leave. Stay in the house. If she doesn't want you here you can leave, but I bet she'll come back needing you."

She as pretty annoyed with him earlier. He wasn't so sure she'd be all excited about seeing him. "Is it that bad?"

"Bad enough to want you around?" Adam laughed with no humor. "Yeah. But I get the feeling she'd like to have you around no matter what."

That's nice Adam felt that way. Ben wasn't so sure about any of that. But there was no way he'd take the chance of disappointing Julie. If she came home needing him, he wanted to be here. "I'll stay."

"Hopefully, she won't start throwing your clothes out of the house."

Ouch. Ben had done that a year ago, when he found out Dale was Cody's father. Adam had been there to see that little show. Not Ben's finest hour. "That's something stupid I would do. Not her."

"Yeah, she's smarter than that." Adam actually smiled. Smartass.

"I'm not going to argue. She's a hell of a lot smarter than I am."

"Aren't they always." Adam nodded toward the house. "Go inside, and I'll go deal with Laramie."

"Good luck."

"Thanks. I'm going to need it." Adam headed for his car. "And Ben, good luck to you."

"I'm going to need it, too." Ben needed to be physically near Julie, even if she wouldn't let him emotionally near her at all. He'd sit and wait for her. And pray he didn't make it worse. And if he did, he'd disappear. For however long she needed.

CHAPTER FIFTEEN

THE SUN WAS long past gone when Joe dropped Julie at Loraine's. Joe and Brook were heading home, and they'd be back in the morning. Which Julie had hoped wouldn't have been necessary.

When they got the last call, she thought—this was it. It couldn't be a false alarm twice. It couldn't.

But it could.

Walking in the police department and seeing the young boy that wasn't her Cody about broke her. His name was Cody, but it wasn't her son. He'd been lost in a mall and the mother still hadn't reached out to the police. How that could even happen still boggled her mind.

And now she was heading into Loraine's house, alone. She'd pushed Ben away. It had been her fault. He'd seen what was playing in her mind. He always had. She didn't want him to know. She didn't want anyone to know she was even considering letting Bettina into Cody's life.

But...

Shit. She didn't know what to do. All she knew was that according to Emily, Bettina was building Fort Knox to keep her family safe—and Julie had done nothing. If she couldn't be trusted with the basics—like his safety—how could she be trusted with the rest of his wellbeing?

Built-up air gushed out of her lungs as she unlocked the front door. Everything was quiet. Joe and Brook had headed back to the city for the night. Allison and Adam were out with another group searching theaters and indoor entertainment centers. They were all working night and day to find Cody, and she couldn't be more appreciative.

Julie dropped her house keys on the table near the door and punched in the code for the security system. She would have to get used to doing that every night. If Cody returned, the security system needed to be used religiously.

No, not if. When. When Cody came back. Because he would. He had to.

She walked into the living room to see who was manning the phone. The desk was empty. But next to the desk sat Ben. Well, not really sitting. He leaned against the back of the chair. His eyes closed. His blond hair disheveled. He looked young and innocent with all the stress gone from his face.

She'd sent him away. Told him to leave. But he hadn't abandoned her this time. He'd stayed. He was a rock. Her rock. She was so lucky he'd come back into her life.

She wanted to let him sleep, but he'd wake up with a starched neck. And heaven forbid he needed to drive anywhere. He wouldn't be able to turn to look out the windows.

Carefully, she shifted a soft blond curl off his forehead. Yeah, his eyes were closed, but he would wake up with a hair dagger poking at his eye. No one ever wanted to wake up like that. Hair daggers were the worst.

That was her story. Don't knock it.

She arranged the hair behind another curl, so it wouldn't fall back down, and his eyes popped open. "Hello," she whispered. She didn't want to scare him.

He looked half asleep, until he didn't. The worry in his eyes was like a blade to the heart. "I'm sorry." He wiped a hand over his eyes. "I didn't mean to fall asleep, but the phone hasn't rung. I turned it up real loud, so I wouldn't miss it. I didn't hear anything. And I would have. I swear."

"Ben, relax. It's okay to fall asleep. There probably won't be anyone calling this late at night anyway."

"Oh, right. But I shouldn't be sleeping." He stood up and stretched out his neck. "I'm the phone guy."

"Thank you for watching the phones, but you're more to me than just the phone guy." Julie needed him to know that.

"I know." He gave her a small smile. "This has been a hard time. I get it."

"No, you don't. Do you know how much more you are to me?"

He shook his head. "No."

"You're my best friend."

He didn't try to hide the cringe.

That cringe struck her right in the gut. "I didn't mean it like that. You're more than just a friend. And I'm so sorry for pushing you away earlier. I was hurt, and mad. And I was taking it out on you. It wasn't fair. You deserve better. And I'm sorry. You don't know how sorry—"

Ben smiled and held out his hand. "It's okay. You had me at hello."

She laughed. An honest to God laugh. It felt good. And nothing had felt this good in what felt like months, even if it was only actually a few days. "Did you just quote *Jerry Maguire*?"

"Did you not quote *Jerry Maguire*?" Ben smiled. "I would think you'd be quoting that movie regularly. 'The human head weighs eight pounds' is a classic."

"'Show me the money'."

"See. So many quotes. And they're so versatile." He wore a big goofy grin.

She hadn't seen him like this in those same few days. "It's nice to see you smile."

"It's nice to hear you laugh." He took one step closer and then another. Slowly inching closer to her.

And she wasn't moving away. In fact, it seemed her feet were bringing her closer to him, too. She needed him. Now, and earlier when she'd dealt with the second nightmare of being so close to Cody and finding she was so far. "I'm sorry I got so mad."

"That's okay. Can I ask you something?"

She didn't know what he wanted to ask, but she was betting she wouldn't like it. "Sure." She tried to say it with confidence, but there wasn't much left.

"At the risk of upsetting you again, did you mean what you said? Do you think your dad was right?"

"I don't know." This was the topic she wanted to avoid. "I just... I don't know what to think. I couldn't keep Cody safe with all the warnings. I made bad choice after bad choice.

"You couldn't have known." Ben stepped closer. His body invading her space. "Do you know why I fell in love with you?"

Her heart thumped and stopped. Just stopped. "You love me?" He loved her. When had that happened? She'd always known she loved him, even when they weren't talking. She always knew her heart was his. But he'd never said the words—not like this— with intensity and the conviction. There was no question.

"Yes. I've loved you for a long time. And do you want to know when I realized you were it for me?" He didn't wait for her to answer. Which was probably best. She'd ruin the moment with sarcasm or insecurity. "It was the first night we'd gone out with Cody. Do you remember? He'd tripped and cut his knee. You gave him that kiss starting at his cut and travelled up his arm. He stopped crying and started laughing. And that was it. Everything was fine. You fixed his entire day. That's a mom."

She did do all of that. And it had been a great night.

"I didn't want him to associate you with a bad time. I was hoping to see more of you, and I didn't want Cody to be unhappy."

"Which is what makes you a great mom." Ben's eyes clouded. "I didn't have a mom like that, so it's nice to see."

"You don't talk much about your parents." Actually, not at all. She'd tried to bring the subject up when they were first together, and he'd change the topic to anything else. Anything. One time he asked about her period rather than talk about his parents. That was some high-level desperation. If this conversation went the feminine hygiene route, she was so out of here.

"My parents aren't something I like to talk about." He laughed, but it obviously wasn't funny. "I'm sure you noticed. Growing up with them wasn't... easy. My mother was an alcoholic and my father was too busy sleeping his way through the secretarial staff to spend time with us. That's when my mom switched to cocaine to numb the pain."

"Did it help?"

"I don't know. She died when I was in second grade." His glance angled down, avoiding her. "I like to think it did—that she was in a better place. I moved in with my Aunt Evelyn and never looked back."

"What about your dad?"

"I saw him on holidays."

"Just on holidays?"

"If I was lucky. He worked a lot." His face went from serious to smiling in seconds. Granted, it was a poor attempt at a smile. "Don't look at me like that. It's not that tragic."

"Look at you like what?"

"Like someone stole my puppy. I had an aunt who loved me, and she took me in no question. She was a better parent than my real parents could have ever been. That's how I know." Ben ran a finger along her cheek, pushing back a wayward hair. But he didn't keep talking.

How would she ever know if he didn't tell her? "Know what?"

"Cody is lucky. The best parent for him is you." The smile on his face slowly morphed from fake-it to make-it. "You are a great mother. You know it. I know it. Cody knows it. That's all that matters."

Her chest warmed. He thought she was a good mother. No. Not good. Great. How many times had her father told her what a failure she was? And how many times had she believed him and kept that narrative rolling her head? Over and over again, she felt his disappointment. Even with him gone, she heard his voice in her head.

But Ben didn't look at her like she was a second-generation train wreck. He didn't pity her for her faults. Just the opposite. He looked at her like she could do no wrong.

She wasn't sure how much she believed it, but it felt really good that he did. And he believed it. She could see the faith he had in her in the intensity of his eyes— the brightness of his smile. She wished she had that much belief in herself.

She dropped her head forward, and her bangs fell into her eyes. "Thank you."

"Nothing to thank me for. I'm just keeping it real." He used one finger to shift her bangs to the side as she lifted her head to stare at him.

How did she get so lucky? Everything about this man made her insides squirm.

"You are amazing." She jumped at him and wrapped her arms around his neck. His arms found her waist and he pulled her to him. He was strong and solid, and his arms kept all her pieces from falling apart.

"I'm glad you think so."

"I do." Tears welled and she blinked them away.

His arms held her tight while he drew his head back and rested his lips on her forehead.

Soft lips. Warm breath. That one kiss meant everything.

His words whispered against her skin. "Why don't you get your pajamas on and I'll be there in a minute. Shay should be here in a few minutes to take over phone duty." He pulled away and she shivered. "And then we'll go to bed. Together."

Go to bed. Yes. That's what she needed. She needed to go to bed and forget today existed. She needed to be here with him and pretend she hadn't nearly lost him or that she was close to losing Cody.

TOO EARLY. Cody didn't want to be up this early. Going to a new school today. That's what *she* told him.

He wanted his old school. And his mommy. *She* even took his Stuffy Puppy.

They were mean.

Mommy Bridgette—that's what she `wanted him to call her—was not like a mommy. Mommies hugged and laughed and sometimes bossed. She just bossed.

"I want to go home." Cody poked his fork at the brown lumps on his plate. She said they were sausage, but they looked weird.

"You are home." Mommy Bridgette huffed as she looked down her nose at him. "This is your new home. You'll learn to like it."

He didn't like it. He'd never like it. This wasn't home.

"Eat your breakfast."

Grass bits sticking out of eggs and weird sausage. This was breakfast? He picked at the scrambled eggs with his fork, but there was green everywhere. He couldn't eat eggs with grass. He wasn't a rabbit. "It's. Green."

"It's organic spinach. It'll make you grow big and strong."

Organic spinach. Another word for grass bits. Gross. He moved the eggs from one side to the other. They didn't get any better looking on the other side of the plate.

"We have to go. It's your first day of school. Eat your food now or you won't eat anything until lunch."

He shrugged. He guessed he wouldn't eat anything. He needed his superpower cereal with marshmallow capes. It made him powerful. He could fly.

And he needed extra marshmallow capes today so he could push the horrible Mommy away and fly home to his real mommy. He needed his superpowers to get back to his real home.

A loud song came from Bridgette's shirt. She pulled a cell phone from some sort of pocket inside her shirt and pressed the button. "Why are you calling me?"

"Change of plans." The lady with the angry voice was on the phone. "Drop him back off at the school and come pick me up."

"At which school?"

"Lincoln."

"Lincoln?" Mommy Bridgette sounded angry too. "And leave him? They'll find him."

"That's the plan."

"Why did we do all of this if we're just going to give him back?"

"Don't question my methods. He's going home."

"I want my mommy." Cody slapped the fork on the plate. He liked the sound.

"Take me off speaker phone. He could recognize my voice."

Mommy Bridgette did something to the phone and the angry lady's voice disappeared. "Fine. But I still get paid the full amount. It's not my fault you changed your mind," Mommy Bridgette yelled into the phone. If she ate less grass she wouldn't be so angry. She clicked off her phone and shoved it back in her shirt. "Go get your stuff. We're leaving."

"Am I going home?" Maybe he didn't need his superpowers.

"Yes. You're going home. Now hurry up."

Cody ran down the hall and grabbed Stuffy Puppy and his backpack from Mommy Bridgette's bed. These were his only things. And going home was the only thing he wanted more.

CHAPTER SIXTEEN

BEN SAT at the kitchen table, lifting his legs as Julie mopped under his feet. "Are you sure you don't want any help?"

"Nope."

He'd tried to help, but she nearly lopped off his head with the mop handle when he'd tried earlier. She was a woman on a mission. And that mission was to mop the finish coat off the tiles. He was starting to question whether their intense make-out session earlier this morning actually happened.

Julie moved to the other side of the table, and Ben put his feet down and picked up his coffee. He hoped it would wake him up. Having Julie in his arms all night made it hard to stay asleep for long.

He wasn't complaining. He loved having her hair brushing his chest. And the soft sighs that came from her lips almost killed him. Those lips were beautiful.

"What?" Julie's was staring at him, the mop on pause. Or better yet, she'd caught him staring at her.

"I was just watching you."

She shook her head, and leaned the mop against the table before crawling underneath the table. Hadn't she cleaned under there already?

"Julie." Adam walked into the kitchen just as Julie crawled out from under the table. "Umm. Were you on the floor?"

"I'm cleaning."

Adam glanced from Ben to Julie, but didn't comment. Instead, he said, "I got a call from Laramie. Cody showed up for school."

"What?" Ben jumped to his feet.

"Can I see him?" Julie didn't smile. Skeptical was the word that came to mind looking at her face. She should be excited. They found Cody.

Dale hadn't gotten the memo. He practically ran in the room. "We have to go."

Julie stood next to the table, looking like she was terrified of getting her hopes up. And she probably was. This would be the third time. "I can't do this again. Are we sure?"

Adam typed into his phone. A second later, it dinged. "Here." He handed the phone to Julie, and she closed her eyes and took a deep breath.

When she opened them, her breath stuttered. "It's him." She ran a finger over the screen.

Adam smiled. "It's him."

"Oh, thank God." Julie's lips slowly curved upward.

Ben looked over her shoulder at the screen. There Cody stood like nothing had happened. "Let's go."

. . .

FIVE MINUTES LATER, they pulled up in front of the school. The building looked the same as when Ben came with Julie, that first day. When all hell broke loose. But even so, there was an edge of something else. Hope. Excitement.

Adam followed Special Agent Laramie down the hall, while Ben, Dale and Julie were ushered into the principal's office. Again with the fucking principal's office. Ben claimed a chair in front of the desk. Dale sat in the chair next to him, but his knee bounced. His hand tapped. The guy was obviously worried about his son.

Cody would like that. The kid needed a father figure, and now he had a father.

"Where is he?" Julie paced back and forth.

"Adam's probably making sure that no hair is out of place. That's my brother though. An anal perfectionist. If he wasn't so annoying about it, it might be funny." Dale looked out the window, lost in his own thoughts, not noticing Julie's previous excitement morphing to anger as they waited longer and longer for the door to open.

Ben hated waiting. Especially when waiting meant bad things. Like it being the wrong kid. Worry skittered over Julie's face. Ben slid his hand in hers and squeezed. "He'll be here." He hoped so, anyway.

She twisted his hand in hers, looking at their combined fingers like they held all the answers to the universe. "You can't know."

"They're probably putting new clothes on him or asking questions." Dale's thumb drummed on his thigh.

Julie pulled her hand away from Ben's and glared at Dale. Ben didn't know all that much about the legal process, but he had some common sense. "They can't ask him questions without a guardian."

"Even so, they're probably bandaging the kid up. He was gone for a while. He might have been hurt depending on how they were keeping him…"

"Shut up!" Julie yelled at the same time Ben screamed, "Enough!"

"What?" Dale looked up in confusion. Every little thing he'd just said made Ben want to scream. He could only imagine how Julie felt.

"Why would someone kidnap him and then send him to school?" Julie sighed. "What if it's another mistake?"

"Adam wouldn't bring you here for a mistake. He was screaming at the police yesterday for all they've put you through." Ben had to believe it. It was all he had right now.

Given the look on her face, Ben could understand why Adam had been yelling.

Heartbreak and worry were clear in her eyes. Her teeth gnawed at her lip. "I just need to see him." Her voice broke.

And Ben about broke as the door swung open and Adam walked in. Alone.

No Cody.

Son of a bitch.

———

JULIE STARED AT THE DOOR. Adam. Just Adam. She couldn't do this again. Please. Please. Please. Not again.

She was not this strong. No one was. "Where is he?"

Her heart hammered in her chest as the world spun. All the stress of the past few days clamped around her throat.

She couldn't breathe. Part of her wondered if her body just gave up. She didn't blame it. She wanted to give up. Crawl into the corner and cry. Just cry.

This was too much. And no one could expect her to be okay.

Adam looked confused "He was being checked out by the EMTs." He turned around. "Come on, bud, your mom is here."

"Mommy?" Cody's voice.

She swore it was Cody's voice. *Thank God.* She stepped around Adam and there he was. "Cody?" She didn't trust her eyes. It looked just like him, but it couldn't be him.

Could it?

Cody ran up to her and wrapped his arms around her waist. Little arms holding tight. She leaned down and kissed his head. Yes. Yes. Yes. This was Cody. Her Cody. She pulled away just long enough to kneel down and pull him close.

He was here. He was okay. Could your heart literally burst from joy?

"I missed you, Mommy."

"I missed you too." There weren't words to describe it. Not that she wanted to describe it. Not with anyone. She wanted to put this behind her.

"The mean mommy made me eat grass."

"Mean mommy?" The person who took him had him call her "Mom"?

"She wasn't nice."

"Well, it's good that you're home, then." Dale stepped up behind Julie.

"Daddy." Cody let go of Julie and ran to his father. Part of Julie wanted to be jealous. But the other part couldn't be jealous when she saw her son's face. He was in heaven.

And if he was in heaven, so was she.

Ben patted Cody's head after he pulled away from Dale. "Good to have you back, kid."

"Hey, Ben." Cody held up a high-five and Ben tapped it. Cody ran into his arms.

"Did you miss us?" Ben asked.

"I did." Cody beamed up at him. The kid loved Ben.

Join the club.

Laramie stepped into the office. "Can we ask him some questions?"

"Sure." Julie was just glad they were here to ask questions of. But doing it at the school? No. She didn't want to be at the scene of the crime any more. She wanted Cody as far away as possible. "Can we do this at the house?"

"Sure." Special Agent Laramie's smile was sympathetic, like she'd heard Julie's inner monologue. That was impossible, though. "But you do know, he'll have to come back here, eventually."

Maybe she had mind-reading abilities. Handy super-power for a cop. Even if it was annoying as hell right now. "I know." She did know, and she had no idea how she was going to send him back to school every day without a cop. Or at least a bodyguard. Or maybe she could quit school— and her job. She'd follow him around like paparazzi followed a movie star.

They'd just have to give up eating and driving and anything else that required money.

"You ready to go home?" Ben asked Cody.

"Yep." Cody nodded, and then his face paled. "Wait." He ran out of the room and Julie turned to go after him.

Ben reached out a hand and stopped her. "He'll be right back."

"You can't know." She didn't want him to leave her sight ever again.

"You can't follow him his whole life." Ben's breath skittered along her neck. Which was strange, since her breath was stuttering in her lungs. She needed Cody back here. She couldn't lose him again.

Before she could move, Cody raced back into the room carrying his backpack and Stuffy Puppy. "I'm ready."

Her breathing returned to normal and she reached out to Cody. Once his hand was in hers, her whole body relaxed. The ramifications of that wasn't something she wanted to think about right now.

She couldn't put him in a bubble or shadow him or handcuff herself to him until college. That wasn't realistic. She'd have to learn to let him go. She'd have to let him out into the world without her.

At some point.

In the future.

Way. Way in the future. Because it wasn't happening today.

Cody skipped next to her as they walked out of the school, and smiled when Ben pulled Julie's keys from his pocket. "Ben's driving your car." His voice was all excitement and happiness. Hearing it again filled her with the same excitement and happiness.

Maybe letting him into the world wasn't going to happen tomorrow, either.

Ben made a face and Cody giggled. Julie opened the back door, and Cody climbed into the back seat and then into his car seat.

Next week wasn't looking good, either. She was so screwed.

CHAPTER SEVENTEEN

"MOMMY BRIDGETTE SAID I was going to a new school, but then the mean voice called and we went to my old school."

"The mean voice?" Julie was so focused on the fact that he was told to call someone else mommy, she almost lost track of the conversation. But then again, they were getting a recount from a five-year-old. Cody was notorious for his wayward stories. Well, not just Cody. All five-year-olds.

"She yelled."

"At you?" Agent Laramie leaned forward in her chair until she was the same height as Cody, but still far enough away to give him room to wiggle and futz with his stuffed dog.

"No, Mommy Bridgette."

"She yelled at Bridgette." Thanks, Agent Laramie, for removing the mommy. That needed to go.

"Yep."

"Why did she yell at Bridgette?"

Cody's shoulders lifted and he shook his head. This was getting nowhere. The kid might be smart as a whip, but he was still a kid.

"What about when your dad dropped you off at school?" Laramie smiled, but Julie could see the frustration. Or maybe that was just her projecting. They weren't any closer to an answer than they were at the beginning of this conversation, and Julie was frustrated as hell.

If the person who'd taken Cody was still out there, how was she going to make sure this didn't happen again without sitting in class with him every day? Okay, time for a different question. "Do you remember that day when Daddy took you to school?"

"Yep." Cody yawned and scrubbed his eyes. The poor kid.

"Where did you go after you went down the slide?"

"In a car."

"Whose car?" Agent Laramie asked, typing on her ever-present tablet.

Cody's shoulders raised again.

"You don't know whose car it was?" Laramie stopped typing and smiled.

He shook his little head, chin nearly on his chest. Like he knew he shouldn't have gotten in the car. And oh, he knew. They'd gone over stranger danger so often. Yet, here they were.

"Why did you get in the car?" Julie might have said that a little too loud. A little angry. Dammit. "You're not in trouble, sweetie." She kneeled next to the chair. "We just want to understand."

"The lady said you were at the hospital, and that I should go with her to see you."

"What lady?" Julie ran a hand along his cheek. "Was it Bridgette?"

He nodded.

Agent Laramie smiled. "Had you seen Bridgette before?"

Cody nodded. That's it. Keep him taking or nodding. As long as Cody stayed engaged he might have something, anything that could shine a penlight on this situation.

"You're doing great." Laramie leaned in. "Was Bridgette the woman who came up to you during hockey practice?"

Cody nodded as he played with the tag on his stuffed dog.

"And she said your mom was in the car?"

Cody made a face and shook his head. "No, she said my mommy was at the hospital."

Julie could understand making bad decisions based on that. Anyone would. Even adults.

Cody yawned. He hadn't taken a nap in years, but the excitement had taken a toll.

Julie made eye contact with Laramie. "Can we finish this later? Cody needs to lay down for a bit."

"I don't want to lay down." Cody yawned, negating the words he'd just said.

"Yeah." Laramie leaned back. "I can come back tomorrow."

"Thanks," Ben said, shaking Laramie's hand. "For everything."

Julie smiled. "I agree. I can't thank you enough."

"Just doing my job." Agent Laramie stuffed her tablet into her bag and hiked it over her shoulder. She picked up the case with the phone equipment they'd broken down earlier and nodded at the pad for the alarm system. "Don't forget that."

Before the front door closed behind her, it swung back open. Allison, followed by Brook, Joe and Loraine, came bursting into the house.

Allison was on Cody before the air swooshed through the front door and hit Julie in the chest. "It is cold out there."

"It's not that bad." True, the sun was high in the sky and the wave of cold spring air wasn't that cold. Even so, Adam was taking his life into his own hands saying that to his bride. Women generally didn't like being contradicted about their feelings. Even if the feelings were just weather-related.

"We've been waiting for you guys to be done for forty-five minutes. Go stand out there and tell me it's not cold." At least that's what it sounded like Allison said. Her face was stuck in Cody's neck.

"No thanks."

"I missed you so much, little guy," Allison murmured.

Cody groaned as she squeezed him. "Auntie Allison, you're killing me."

"Don't break his bones." Brook came up behind

Cody and joined in on the hug. "I need some of that love too."

"Oh wait, it's a group thing?" Joe jumped in, followed by Adam.

Poor Cody was the center of a tightly knit burrito, and Julie didn't want to stop the love fest. That didn't mean she wanted him juiced like that kid in the Wonka chocolate factory. "Okay, everyone. It's time for Cody to lie down for a bit."

One by one, family and friends unwrapped their arms from his little body. Once he was outside the cocoon, Loraine walked over.

"Cody, my favorite grandson." Loraine bent down and lifted him from the ground. "Don't ever do that to me again. I'm an old woman."

"I won't, Grandma."

"Good boy." She kissed his cheek. "Now take a nap and I'll make you your favorite dinner when you wake up."

"Macaroni and cheese?"

"Yep." Loraine set Cody down. "Now let's go take a quick nap."

"Okay." He ran up to Dale. "Will you help Grandma put me to bed?"

"Sure, buddy." Loraine, Dale and Cody bounded up like nothing had changed. But everything had changed.

"What the hell happened? Where was he?" Allison sat on the couch. So much for pleasantries. They wanted to know what was going down.

Julie couldn't blame them. "We received a call this morning that Cody was at his school."

"They just dropped him off? No demand? Nothing?" Brook sat next to her sister.

"Nothing." Adam sighed.

Yep. Julie felt that sigh in her soul. She didn't like the whole nothing thing either.

"What did they want?" Allison huffed.

Julie could understand that whoosh all too well. "We don't know. Her name is Bridgette. At least we think that's her name. She made Cody call her Mommy Bridgette."

"If she made him call her Mommy, why did she bring him back?"

"We don't know." Adam shook his head. "The local cops are just as confused as we are. There were no ransom demands, nothing. They just took him back to school."

"What did Cody have to say?"

Julie groaned. "He's five. What do you think he said? They fed him grass, which after further discussion turned out to be spinach in eggs. And there was a mean voice on the phone."

Adam sat on the edge of the couch, next to Allison. He looked about as skeptical as Julie felt. "Bridgette. Who the hell could that be? No distinguishing characteristics. Nothing."

Don't get her wrong, Julie was happy they found Cody. Her lungs felt freer. Her body looser. But without some of these questions answered, there was always the chance for a repeat. These were the hardest few days of her life. And she couldn't do a rerun. "So what do we do now?"

"Now that Cody is found, the local cops will keep investigating, but there's not much to go on." Adam held on to his wife's hand as he shook his head. "We'll have to increase security. We have the security system here and at your cottage, but I want to do more."

"What else can be done?" Ben was behind Julie. Really close. She liked it.

"Motion detectors. And I thought about having a gate installed." Adam couldn't honestly be thinking of locking down the house like that. Loraine would hate it.

"I don't want to put Loraine out like that." Julie wanted Cody safe, but how far would they go? "That doesn't help when I have to drop him off at school. We can't keep him safe there."

"There's private school," Brook said, not looking at Julie. Something was up. "One of the partners at my law firm sends his kids to a school on the north side of Chicago."

"How much does that run?"

"The cost doesn't matter. We can help." Allison wouldn't meet Julie's eyes either. They were all in on this.

"I'm not taking anyone's money," Julie told them.

"Did your dad leave you anything?" Joe asked. He looked around as they all stared at him. "What?" He must not have gotten the memo that her father only left her money if she abandoned her son.

Brook patted his arm. "Oh, honey. We'll talk."

"I take it that's a no," Joe said.

"No," Julie confirmed. Most normal people wouldn't even consider that a father would put a stipulation like that in their will. Leave it to Edward Connolly to be the shadiest, shittiest man on the block. Even in death.

"Julie." Allison leaned forward. "It's not charity. We're not offering it to you. We're offering Cody a scholarship to a private school. The parents are foreign dignitaries and celebrities. Not just anyone can walk in the door."

Every part of her body wanted to say yes, but this wasn't healthy. She couldn't just uproot him from his classes. Not like this. Not based on fear. "I'll think about it." She had to think about it. Because even though she didn't want to make a kneejerk decision, this could be Cody's chance. Peace of mind of for her, knowing he was in a safer, more secure environment. And he'd be challenged. It could be a win-win.

But something deep inside her wasn't sure that was the answer.

And she wasn't sure why.

FOUR HOURS LATER, the sun was down and the family was up. The noise was deafening as everyone talked and laughed. They'd gone so long without a happy moment, everyone was taking full advantage. Everyone stuck around for dinner. Whether it was hanging with Cody or the promise of Loraine's macaroni and cheese, Ben wasn't sure.

He was sure though that it was a cozy *family* moment—and he felt out of place.

"Dad, can you play this with me?"

"Sure, kiddo." Dale sank down on the rug, where Cody had already set up the Mousetrap game. The one with all the pieces that had to be put together. Ben should have been surprised the kid did it on his own. But this was Cody. Nothing really surprised him anymore.

"How do you play?" Dale asked.

"You put the mouse here, and then you turn the handle." Of course, Cody was still a kid and had no desire to actually play the game. He just wanted to play with the complicated mousetrap. Ben couldn't really blame him. The game was fun. Catching little plastic mice was just a bonus.

Dale turned the handle, and Cody bounced in place when Dale's mouse was caught. "I got you."

The whole point of the game was that you slowly built the trap and if anyone made a mistake—even a little— the trap might not work. But Cody always built the trap and it always worked. From the first time he'd put it together, without help, to now.

"I win," Cody shouted.

"But I didn't even get to do anything. How did you win?" Dale was pretending to pout. At least Ben thought it was pretend. If it wasn't, that was just sad. Ben would go with pretending.

"You put your mouse there. I win. Want to play again?"

"So, if I didn't put my mouse there, I would have won?"

"No."

"So then, how do I win?" Dale sounded legitimately confused. They'd all been there. Playing with Cody could be interesting. He didn't like to lose. And because of his ability to figure things out, he generally didn't.

"Umm…" Cody stared at the game board.

"Why would I want to play again if there's no way for me to win?" Dale pointed out. Ben gave him credit for trying.

Cody moved his piece over to the other side of the board. "Mom, pick a color."

"Why?" Julie came in from the kitchen, carrying a glass of water. She wasn't letting herself get too far from Cody. Which was cute, except when Ben thought about her job. She couldn't take him to work with her. And she couldn't go to school with Cody. Something was going to have to give, and when it did it would be painful.

Cody pointed at the mice. "Pick a color so we can trap you."

"No way." Julie shook her head. "I don't want to lose."

"Uncle Adam?"

"I'm busy, buddy," Adam called from the kitchen, where he stood over a giant pot of boiling water, dumping in multiple boxes of elbow macaroni. Water splashed over the side, making him flinch, and the women in the kitchen laughed.

"Ben?"

"Sure. I'll play."

Cody bounced up and down. "What color?"

"Yellow."

"I'll put your mouse right here." Cody flopped onto the rug and stuck Ben's mouse under the trap. "Here it goes."

All the pieces moved, but when the mousetrap fell, it stopped before it hit the board.

"Why didn't it work?" Cody scowled and poked at the trap. He threw a mouse and landed a fist on the board. "What is wrong with you?"

Whether the kid was talking to the game or to himself, Ben wasn't sure. Either way, it wasn't good.

Julie put down her drink. "Cody, breathe."

"But it doesn't work." He yanked one of the pieces out. "It's supposed to work."

"Cody." Julie moved to his side and grabbed his hand. "We talked about this. Breathe."

"I am breathing or I'd be dead."

"Cody!"

"Fine." Cody closed his eyes and put his hands in his lap. He took a deep breath. When his eyes opened, the storm had passed. "I'm back to normal."

"You're always normal, sweetheart. We just have to remember to breathe." Julie smiled as she ran a hand down Cody's cheek. "This is a toy. Nothing to get upset over."

Cody nodded. And just like that, Julie proved she was the perfect mother for Cody.

Ben's heart beat a little faster, hoping things didn't change now that Cody was back and Dale was vying for Father of the Year. Because there was no way he'd come between a boy and his father. He'd lived without a father and wouldn't wish that on anyone. Especially Cody.

CHAPTER EIGHTEEN

BEN HAD NEVER BEEN SO full in his life. With all the cheese and carbs in his system, he was on the verge of a food coma. And it was so worth it. Loraine's cooking was amazing. It reminded him of his aunt's. Evelyn had always made everything from scratch. She canned jellies and preserves. Times like this, he really missed her.

Allison was currently driving the conversation, keeping things light. "How are you both settling into the new house?"

"It's been interesting, but we're almost done painting the inside." Shay smiled. "Having my brother home would come in handy." Shay's brother was studying at NYU. Letting him go had been hard, but her boyfriend Garret kept Shay busy. She seemed to be handling it pretty well.

"How's he liking college?" Brooke leaned her head on Joe's shoulder.

"He loves it. He's already talking about getting an

apartment with a group of friends and staying there year-round."

"How do you feel about that?"

"Part of me is happy that he's acclimated so well. The other part wants him to hate it so much he wants to come home." Shay shook her head. "That's horrible. I don't want him to hate it. Just come home."

"I can't even imagine when that day will come." Julie dropped her forehead onto her arm, resting on the table.

Ben slid his hand up and down her back. Getting Cody to kindergarten tomorrow was going to be hard enough without worrying about twelve years from now. Not that he was going to say that out loud. He didn't think it would offer her the comfort he'd think the sentiment should.

On the other side of Julie, Cody yawned and laid his head on the table. They'd been sitting here talking for a while. Anything to show Cody everything was normal. Nothing to remind him of the past couple days. And Cody had bounced around, taking it all in. Until now.

"Time for bed, buddy." Julie stacked Cody's plate on hers.

"Leave that. My boys will clean up." Loraine shooed Julie away. "Go put the boy to bed."

"Are you sure?" Julie aimed the question at Adam, but when it came to his mother, he'd do anything to help her, and Loraine would do anything to help those around her.

"Apparently, I'm sure." Adam added Julie and

Cody's plates to the stack in front of him and turned to Loraine. "Go with Allison into the living room. We'll do the dishes. Right, Dale?"

Dale sighed but nodded.

Julie slid her hand in Cody's. "Come on, little man. Time for bed."

"I don't want to go to bed." If his face wasn't planted on the wooden table, it might be more believable. As it was, the kid was practically asleep already.

"Okay, then let's get your pajamas on and we'll talk about it. Would you like to say goodnight to everyone?"

"Goodnight." Cody ran a fist over his eyes. There wasn't going to be any talking about anything if his half-lidded eyes had anything to say about it.

As Julie led Cody up the stairs, the conversation in the kitchen turned to wine and dessert.

"I made a batch of chocolate cookies for the county food bank bake sale. I packed the extras in a container in the pantry." Loraine took her glass over to the sink and yawned. "It's been a long day. I'm going to head upstairs. You all are welcome to spend the night. No one drive home drunk."

"You're in a room full of cops," Adam said. "We're not going to let anyone drive drunk."

Loraine planted a kiss on Adam's cheek. "Just show everyone to a room if they need one."

"I will." Adam held his dripping hands over the sink while she held him close.

After Loraine left, the conversation moved on to police procedure and cases. It was enough for Ben to lose interest and wonder what was taking Julie. It was boring enough that he excused himself and headed up the stairs.

He stopped at Cody's door when he heard her voice. "Go to sleep, Cody, and I'll see you tomorrow."

Ben moved to the other side of the hallway just as Julie appeared in the doorway. She jumped, and Ben put a finger to his lips before she could yell out. *Sorry,* he mouthed as she shut the door.

"What are you doing up here?" She led him down the hall, away from Cody's door.

"I just wanted to check on you."

"Did you miss me?" Julie ran her hands along his arms and slid them behind his back. Her body pressed against his.

Did he miss her? Well, that was obvious. "Yes."

She shimmied, ever so slowly and it lit Ben's body on fire. She was soft and warm. And every shift in her body made him want to take her to her bedroom and celebrate that today was a very good day.

Her lips found his. Soft and sweet. She was everything, wrapped into one perfect package. And she was here with him.

Her hands roamed lower and thoughts about anything floated from his mind. Her fingers were strong as they pulled him closer. And all he wanted was to be closer. Her lips teased. Her hands clawed. Soft and sweet was long gone. She was desperate. Needy. And dammit did he need. He needed her.

"Mom?"

Julie flew back. Ben's body probably turned a horrible shade of blue. Or it might have just been his balls. Either way, the air around him chilled and he missed having her in his space. His body throbbed.

But Cody needed her. She opened his bedroom door and put on the light. "Are you okay, Cody?"

"Yeah. Where's Stuffy Puppy?"

"I think he's by your school bag." She looked at Ben, and he willed his body to take the hint.

Ben readjusted himself as he whispered, "I'll check" before running down the stairs. Stuffy Puppy was exactly where Julie said, and Ben came back up and handed the dog to Julie. He leaned against the wall and breathed, thinking about anything that would stop his blood from throbbing in his veins.

Kissing sounds and giggles came from the bedroom. "I'm going to tuck you in tight. Snug as a rug in a jug."

"Good night, Mommy."

"Good night, baby."

The bedroom light dimmed as Julie walked out. "We should head downstairs before he comes out and catches us. I already need to get him into therapy because of the past few days. I can't afford more sessions from seeing his mom in a compromising position."

"Let's go." He tried to smile, but sharing her with the people downstairs after getting all amped up was not his idea of fun.

"Hold on." Julie stopped. "Will you stay here tonight?"

"Are you sure?" He shouldn't be discussing this right now, but he couldn't seem to stop himself. "He might see us."

"I'm sure. If he sees us, we'll explain. Might as well get our money's worth from the therapist." She shook her head. "He might not even notice." She seemed so sure of herself. He didn't have the heart to remind her that kids notice everything.

If she wanted to live in denial, that was okay for now. He wasn't exactly an expert on handling stress. The past year taught him that. Well, the past year and his therapist. Speaking of. "Do you think you might want to see a therapist?" He knew he was pushing it, but she mentioned it first. And he couldn't think of a better time to get it out there.

Her eyes narrowed, and her mouth flattened. His mouth went into overdrive. "I'm not saying you need it or anything, just that you might want to consider talking to someone about the past few days." He was totally fucking this up. "It would be hard for anyone. Not that it's hard for you." She was never going to talk to him again, and would he blame her? He was rambling like an ass, telling her she couldn't handle her shit. "Can you talk, so I'll stop?" His mouth closed— maybe indefinitely. He couldn't put his foot in it if it was shut.

A small smile touched her lips. "It's fine. I'll think about it. How's that?"

"Good." He reached out and waited till she put her hand in his. "Let's go downstairs and see what they're talking about."

"Probably me and Cody."

"Probably."

They walked down the stairs hand in hand, and

Ben felt light. They were all safe. Julie wanted him here. And they could finally put everything from the past few days behind them. Finally.

IF JULIE WASN'T SO interested in the loud discussion downstairs in the living room, and what it meant in terms of catching whoever abducted Cody, she'd be enjoying the feeling of Ben's hand in hers.

As it was, the silence that followed Adam saying, "You left Russia, and divorced your Russian bride. How can you be sure there's no Russian connection?" kept her thoughts hostage. Dale had a habit of bringing drama back whenever he came home.

"Nadia and I have been living in Costa Rica for the past year," Dale said as Julie and Ben crossed the living room "I didn't leave her. She left me, for some plastics billionaire with a vacation home on the coast."

"That sucks." Allison might have slurred the word a bit. But then again, she'd just downed a huge gulp of wine.

Dale nodded. "Thanks. But it was for the best. She wanted things I didn't want."

"Like?"

"Kids. Marriage. Staying in one place." Dale laughed, but he obviously didn't think it was funny.

Allison used her free hand to draw a circle in the air next to her ear. "How crazy of her to want those things."

"It wasn't crazy. Coming back, almost losing Cody

—I want those things too, I don't think I wanted them with her."

"Harsh."

"Maybe. But when I realized I wasn't happy, I didn't jump into the first warm bed I could find." Dale exhaled sharply. "I can't even blame her. She must have known something wasn't right. And it wasn't. She just left before I did."

"So if it's not the Russians, who could it be?" Julie took the only empty seat, next to Dale on the couch. The chairs were all filled with her friends. The celebratory vibe had disappeared, and now everyone was back in detective mode. It helped they had three detectives in the room.

"I still go back to someone wanting to shake you down for money." Garret made a lot of sense. But there was an obvious flaw with the ransom theory.

"I have no money." Julie wasn't destitute. She and Cody had everything they needed, mostly because she lived rent-free in Loraine's cottage. Everything she made went to her car payment, school, and day-to-day expenses. Ransom-worthy money just wasn't there.

"Maybe they didn't know," Garret suggested.

Shay shook her head. "We're missing something. Has anything changed lately? Anything new happen?"

Julie shrugged. "My father died."

"What about someone from the funeral?" Shay asked.

Ben turned to Julie. "Didn't Mrs. Smith lose a grandson?"

"She wouldn't be looking for money." Julie shook

her head. The Smiths had more money than she would see in a lifetime.

"Well, people always need money, but maybe she was looking for another grandson," Ben said—and then winced when she gave him a look. Even he had to see the ridiculousness of that statement.

The idea was absolutely ridiculous. The Smith children played with Julie when they were kids. They'd spent the night at each other's houses, watching Nickelodeon and building couch forts. And the children had grown and moved away, but that didn't mean Mrs. Smith would try to take Cody. Could it?

"She's a family friend." Adam spoke up with so much certainty, Julie almost believed him. "She sees my mother at least once a week. She was just over at her house a couple nights ago for book club. There's no way she could hide him from us, even if she wanted to."

Shay nodded. "Like I said, we're missing something."

"We have to be," Adam agreed. "Maybe I'll go visit Laramie tomorrow and see if there's something in the file."

"We should probably go." Shay stretched her arms over her head. "You didn't drink, right?"

Garret smiled and jingled keys. "Anyone need a ride to the city?"

Allison raised her hand. "I gotta work tomorrow." She stumbled to her feet. She'd definitely dipped a little too deep into the wine bottle. "You." She pointed at Julie, then Ben. "You are both off tomorrow."

"The Mesko design?"

"I got it. I got it all." Allison waved her arms. "I'm an independent woman."

"You're amazing." Adam wrapped his arms around her. "Maybe we should stay here tonight."

"But work?" There was a hint of desperation—or maybe it was the wine.

Adam stared at her and smiled. "Okay, I'll drive you home."

"That's why I married you." Allison smiled and grabbed the half-full wine bottle. "I'm ready."

"Whoa, Busta Rhymes. Drop the Courvoisier." Adam slid the bottle out of Allison's hands. "Leave this here."

"You're no fun." Allison giggled, and Adam tickled her while she tried to reach for the bottle again.

"Let's get you home before you pass out." Arm around her waist, Adam led her to the front door.

"Don't come to work," Allison yelled. "Garret, shoot them if they try to come in."

"Sure," Garret said, then he turned to Ben and shook his head.

Brook laughed as Allison tripped over Adam's feet. "Good luck getting her home." She dragged Joe out his seat by one hand, and walked out the front door, after Adam and Allison, followed by Shay and Garret.

Ben shut the front door and Julie armed the security system.

"You ready to go to bed?" Ben asked.

"Yes." Julie wanted to get Ben into bed so bad. The house was secure and everyone safe. "But I'm not tired."

"You're not?" Ben's eyes widened.

"Not at all." She smiled and shimmied her hips as she walked toward the stairs. Not looking back. She knew he'd follow. He'd follow her anywhere, although he didn't need to. She'd follow him to the ends of the earth. Hopefully she'd never find a reason to.

CHAPTER NINETEEN

JULIE LAY IN BED. Awake. Wide awake, with little chance of catching any Zs. Ben was snoring, but that wasn't why she couldn't sleep. Every creak and bump sent her mind racing. Was someone in the house? Was Cody somehow getting out of the house?

She'd tried everything. The sheep had been counted. She'd told herself a bedtime story about a woman who couldn't sleep—her imagination was tired, sue her.

The house settled with a loud crick and she sat up in bed. The bed dipped. She was going to wake Ben. She didn't want to wake him up. He was sleeping for both of them at this point.

She stared at the closed door as Ben snored. She needed to see Cody. Just once.

Julie slid out of bed, taking her time, peeling the blanket inch by inch off her body. She angled her legs toward the floor and scooted forward. Stood up.

She tiptoed across the room and opened the door. One little moan came from the hinge before it fell silent. Ben kept snoring. She eased out the door and into the dark hallway.

All was quiet. No settling. No one moving around. Downstairs wasn't lit up—no one manning phones. The house was tired. Quiet. The silence wrapped around Julie, making it hard to breathe.

Cody. She needed to see Cody.

She stopped at his door. Just stopped. She was exhausted. Maybe she'd made the whole thing up and Cody wasn't in his bed.

She couldn't. Not again.

A twist of the knob and she'd be sure. She opened his door. Groan. Squeak. The hinges did everything but send up flares to announce her arrival.

His little head was at the bottom of the bed. His hair in exclamation points. He looked so peaceful. And so home. Every part of her heart hurt. Not in sadness. In joy. She'd never known how much she loved that kid until he wasn't there. He was her soul. Without him her heart didn't beat.

He didn't wake as she came closer. One step after another along the carpet.

Cody turned on his side, leaving the left side of the bed empty. He subconsciously wanted her to stay. At least that's what she was going with, if anyone asked. Anyway, she wasn't going to stay in bed with him all night. Just a minute. Just to make sure he was real.

She took a pillow laid it at next to Cody's head.

Taking a spare blanket from the back of the chair in the corner, she draped it over Cody before sliding in next to him.

Cody mumbled in his sleep. Julie smoothed a piece of his hair back. She hadn't slept in the same bed with Cody since he was three and thought there were monsters in his closet. That had been a nice phase.

Not because he was scared of his closet and wouldn't go inside without her around. That sucked. But it was one of the more cuddly phases. A *Mom can you stay with me* phase.

It sure beat the *no* phase when he was two and a half. Cody, time for bed— No. Cody, clean your room— No. Everything was no. Including her decision to give up carbs. That lasted two days in the *no* phase.

But the *monster in the closet* phase transformed her into a hero. She would open the closet door armed with a whiffleball bat. And he'd look at her like she was Spiderman saving the planet. It was nice. Then he got older and the monsters disappeared.

Don't get her wrong, she was glad the monsters went away. Checking your thirty-year-old son's room for monsters would not be okay. But it was nice while it lasted.

She curved her arm over Cody's body and her eyes closed. She'd stay here a few minutes. That's all.

"DID YOU SLEEP, BUDDY?" Julie heard Ben's voice before her eyes opened. She must have fallen asleep.

"Yep."

"What about your mom?"

"I don't know." Cody's voice was nearby, but not in the bed. He must have gotten up.

"What are you doing?"

"Getting ready for school."

"You're not worried about going to school?"

"Nope." Cody sounded so sure of himself. Too bad Julie wasn't feeling as strong.

"We should wake up your mom before you go anywhere."

School? Julie's eyes flew open. Cody was on the floor, putting on his socks. He'd already put on his jeans and a sweater. He'd dressed himself. Which was adorable since sometimes it took bribery to get him to take care of business in the morning. But today was different.

"You're not going to school today," Julie said, voice scratchy.

"Why?" Cody sounded so confused, like he went to school every day, so why not today Which was all true. But after yesterday and the things running through her mind... She was terrified someone else would take him. She was worried he'd wander off— or get hurt—or get beaned by a rogue meteorite. It was bad enough she was afraid for him to leave the house. If she told him any of that, then he'd be afraid. And he deserved better.

Julie pretended to smile. "I just think it would nice to spend time together today."

"But Mom, I have to play scientists with Toby."

"Scientists?"

"Yep. Toby's birthday present. Remember?"

"Sounds exciting." She did remember. The day he'd disappeared, the boys were going to play with the set. "Could we invite him over for a playdate this weekend and you could play scientist?"

"Okay." Cody bounced up and down. "I'll tell him today."

At school. He didn't say it, but the implication felt like a nail to her heart.

She wanted to put her foot down. *You will not go to school.* But at some point, he'd have to go back.

Ben sat on the bed next to Julie as Cody ran to the closet and threw open the door. They hadn't brought all his toys in from the house, but they'd brought a few. Cody pulled out a plastic safety glasses from a set she'd bought him last year. "I'll bring this."

She smiled at the excitement in his eyes, but she couldn't let him go. Not yet. "Didn't you put your magnifying glass in your bag already?" The day he hadn't made it to school. The day she couldn't relive. She couldn't let him go. Maybe if she kept him talking he'd forget.

"Yeah, but you can use a magnifying glass and goggles. I'm gonna put them in my school bag." And he was gone. All the excitement sucked from the air as he left.

"It will be okay." Ben laced his fingers through hers. "You have to let him go eventually."

"I could homeschool him."

"You could. But then how would he play scientist with Toby?"

"Freaking Toby." She groaned and pushed her face into the pillow. She actually used freaking when talking about another five-year-old.

"Freaking Toby is his friend. And it's good he has friends. And it's good for Cody to get out of the house and learn new things."

All this logic was pissing her off. "I'm not ready," she muttered into the pillow. She didn't want Ben to hear it, anyway. It was embarrassing to admit she wasn't ready to let her son be normal. Not yet. Later. Much later.

"It's not about you."

Damn logic. "I know." She emerged from the pillow. Cody deserved some normal after all the trauma. And he didn't seem traumatized. He seemed okay. She should be dancing a jig—super happy tCody wasn't balled up in a corner begging to never leave the house.

And she was happy—about that. Just not about letting him go. Because who knew what would happen when he went to the school. Alone? Who knew who'd be there waiting? She didn't have the strength to find out.

———

BEN RAN a finger over Julie's palm, trying to erase the worry from her eyes. "If you don't let him go school today, it's not going to get easier tomorrow. It'll be harder."

"Fine." She rolled onto her back. "Why is this so hard?"

"I don't know?" And Ben had no idea why it was hard, only that it was. He was putting on a brave face, but honestly, he wanted to shadow that kid every step of his day today. "All I know is that kid is fearless."

"Right? What the hell is wrong with him? He should be afraid or something. I'm terrified and I can't say anything to him because he's just taking it all in stride."

"They say kids are more resilient."

"Pfft." She grabbed both ends of the pillow and wrapped it around her head. "Kids are too dumb yet to know how much life sucks."

"Do you want to be the one who teaches him? We could keep him here."

"No." She let go of the pillow and sat up. "The world will do that soon enough."

"Mom!" Cody came into the room. "When are we leaving?"

"I can take you, buddy." Ben looked at Julie and whispered, "If it would be easier."

"No." Cody planted himself in front of Julie. The fear in his eyes was new. It might not be overpowering, but the trauma from the past few days was there, inside him. "You have to take me."

"Okay." Julie nodded and smiled, feeling like a bobblehead. "Let me put on some clothes and I'll make you breakfast."

"Grandma's making eggs." Cody ran to the door and turned around. "You'll take me to school, right?"

"I'll be down in a few minutes." Julie nodded. Again. "Are you sure you're okay going to school today?"

Cody didn't say anything for a few seconds. He truly seemed to be thinking about the question. "Yep. You get me to school." He didn't ask. It was more like a statement of fact. That she was trusted to get him there without issue.

"I can."

"Good." The kid's smile lit up the room before he disappeared.

Julie sighed. "Well, so much for no trauma."

"It's not as bad as it could be."

"That kid is still my hero." She swung her legs off the bed. "I have to get dressed, and somehow figure out how to drop him off at school without having a breakdown."

"Want some company?"

"Thank goodness, yes. I didn't want to presume, but I can use all the help I can get." She stopped at the doorway. "Wait. Aren't you going into work?"

"You heard Allison. Garret's supposed to shoot us."

"True, but there's no way she's going to be able to handle everything today. She's probably still passed out."

"I texted her. She's miserable, but awake." He leaned in and dropped a kiss to her cheek. Her skin was soft, and the way she melted with the touch warmed his body all over. "I'm all yours today."

She grabbed his hand and led him out of Cody's room, straight to hers. They both got dressed. Cool and calm. They could do this. They could do this together. And no matter what, he'd be there to help her with whatever she needed.

CHAPTER TWENTY

JULIE TOOK the pages Ben handed her. The three of them—her, Ben and Adam—had been poring over the file Adam got from Detective Barrows for hours. Agent Laramie wasn't into sharing—probably an FBI thing. Since Barrows had started the investigation, he had accumulated quite a bit of paperwork. Despite Cody only being gone for a few days, they had more information than one person could get through in a week.

She looked at the current file. *Cody's mother seemed distraught. Subject paced and fidgeted.* "I suppose there are worse things to be thought of than distraught." Julie sipped her coffee. She was close to needing a refill.

"They document the family just in case it's a hoax," Adam said.

Ben said the words Julie was thinking. "A kidnapping hoax? What kind of crazy person would do that? Why?"

Adam shook his head. "Attention."

"That sounds terrible." Understatement of the century. Julie couldn't even imagine pretending her child was kidnapped. How would that even work. And why?

"There's a lot of terrible people out there," Adam said, as if they were talking about crappy fast food and not putting a child through hell. "What time do you have to pick up Cody?"

"I'm not picking him up." Julie tried to keep her voice even—like it was no big deal that she wasn't going to be the first to see him walk out that door. "We've decided to get everything back on schedule so Cody doesn't think things are different. Your mother's picking him up."

"Are you okay with that?" Adam looked up.

"I have to be." She couldn't let Cody see her sweat. He had to get back to normal. "I need him to not be afraid."

"But you're afraid." Adam didn't ask, just said it as a fact. Which it was.

"That's unavoidable. But I can try to keep it from Cody. Try to give him a normal life—until it gets back to normal. For real."

"Were you ever normal?" Ben didn't smile. He looked so serious...except for the sparkle in his eye.

Jerk. "Hey!" She punched his arm.

Ben laughed. "What? Honest question."

She knew what he was doing. Still a jerk, even if the mood seemed somehow lighter. Which was impressive given what they were sifting through.

"Okay, I've never been normal." Julie laughed and

finished her coffee. If she was going to go at this box again after Cody went to bed, she was going to need a lot more caffeine. "We should probably put this away before Cody gets home."

"How much time do we have?"

"About ten minutes." She stacked papers in a pile at the side of the table as the front doorbell dinged.

"Are you expecting anyone?" Ben checked his watch.

Julie didn't bother. Loraine should be home soon, but it was a little too early and she wouldn't ring her own doorbell. The only reason Julie could think of was something had happened to Cody.

"I got it." Julie jumped up, ignoring the look of terror in Ben's eyes. She needed to be there first.

She reached the door and twisted the knob. The door opened. No uniform. Not a cop. Her breath whooshed out.

Her father's girlfriend, Bettina stood on the front porch. Loraine's front porch. In front of Julie. Bettina's white cashmere coat was wrapped tight around her body, with a matching white silk scarf wrapped around her neck. Her dyed-blonde hair was pulled taut in a bun on her head. Maybe she'd be less bitchy if her hair wasn't pulled so tight. That couldn't be good for the scalp.

"Good afternoon, Miss Connolly. Proper protocol dictates a greeting." Even though Bettina was shorter than Julie, she still managed to peer down her nose at her. It must be a gift.

Julie's voice materialized. "Hello?"

"That sounded like a question, but it was a statement."

"It was. What are you doing here?" That was a question.

"It's pleasure to see you, too," Bettina said. "Nice house. Albeit too far from the city." She sniffed the air, nose scrunched. "Is that cows?"

There was a working farm over a mile away from the house. On hot days in middle of July, you could catch the scent of cow pies. But on a cold day in the middle of the spring, not so much. Unless, of course, you were Bettina Wilcox.

She had the nose of a bloodhound and the disposition of one of those spoiled little yappy fluffy dogs. Too bad she didn't have cute floppy ears and a lolling tongue. Then maybe it wouldn't be an absolute nightmare dealing with her.

"Have you completely forgotten your manners? Are you going to let me in?" Bettina tried to look through the doorway, but Julie blocked the way.

Julie wasn't buying any of this. "Can't forget what you never had." As far as her father was concerned, she'd never had manners. Might as well own it.

"Regardless, may I come in. I'm in a bit of hurry and we need to talk."

"About?" Julie didn't bother moving. She wasn't excited about continuing whatever this was.

Bettina glared. Just glared. But it was obvious she wasn't going to leave until they talked. Might as well get it over with.

Julie stepped to the side. "Please come in."

Bettina nodded and walked in the door. No. She didn't walk. She sashayed. She was too classy to walk like the plebes. "Hello, Detective Byrnes."

"Ms. Wilcox." Adam walked over with an outstretched hand. Ever the gentleman.

"Benjamin Mooring."

"Ms. Wilcox." Ben shook her hand. Another gentleman. And they said chivalry was dead. Oh wait, it was only Bettina's cold heart that was dead.

Bettina turned to Julie. "I need to speak with you."

"Okay." This was ridiculously formal, even for Bettina. "Please sit." Julie was going to sit. They should all sit. She took one end of the couch.

"Thank you." Bettina descended slowly onto the opposite end of the couch, unwrapping her silk scarf and draping it across the coffee table. "We need to talk alone."

Fantastic. Adam dumped the paperwork on the coffee table into the box and closed the lid. "I'll be in the kitchen."

Ben looked at Julie, silently asking if he should leave the room. She nodded and he picked up her coffee cup. "I'll be right in the kitchen, getting you that refill." He said it as a threat, but Bettina was too busy unbuttoning her coat to notice.

Both men disappeared, leaving her alone with Bettina. Maybe this was a mistake.

Bettina settle back against the cushions. "I heard that you found Cody."

"I did." She didn't want to get into this with Bettina. Or anyone for that matter. She didn't need to hear how bad a mother she was. She'd heard that enough in her own mind.

Bettina reached out and laid her hand on Julie's. "I'm so happy that he's safe." The words were kind. The face matched. It was almost like she was speaking the truth. Like Bettina had been concerned for Cody and Julie. It was disconcerting seeing Bettina as a human. "I was so afraid when I heard he'd gone missing."

"Me too." Julie felt those words to her core. Afraid was just the tip. Terrified. Destroyed. Not something she ever wanted to relive.

"How did you survive not knowing where he was?"

"It was hard." Talking about it was reliving it. She was not about to go into more detail. Not now. Or ever. Time for a subject change. "What are you doing here?" Not that she wanted to talk about that, either.

Bettina never wanted anything good.

"Straight to the point." Bettina shifted in her seat. She seemed uncomfortable. She was never uncomfortable. She was always ice. "I wanted to apologize for that stipulation in your father's will."

"Stipulation?"

"The payout." Bettina shook her head. "No mother would ever walk away from their child. Not a good mother. And you are a good mother."

The woman had never said anything remotely nice about Julie. Ever. This was—nice—no, weird, but in a nice way.

"He only had the best of intentions for Cody," Bettina said.

His intentions were cruel. "My father never wanted what was best for Cody. He only cared about himself."

A flash of anger crossed Bettina's face before her lips turned up in a fake smile. "We will agree to disagree. Either way, Cody is a gifted boy. He needs to be mentally stimulated and challenged."

The words from the letter pulsed in Julie's head. *Extricate yourself from his life. Bettina will raise him...*

"I only want what's best for the boy. I'll pay for him to go to a private school in New York. I have a friend on the board who said they can get him in in the middle of the term. They have a room available, and you can see him on weekends and breaks."

Weekends and breaks?

"I see you have concerns." Bettina pulled an envelope from her pocket. "This details the programs they offer and the security requirements. There are three diplomatic families and a few celebrities whose children attend the school. They need high-level security."

When Julie wouldn't take the envelope, Bettina laid it on the coffee table. "I know this is hard, but it's for the best. The school can ensure his safety."

Because Julie couldn't. She couldn't keep him safe.

"You need to go." Ben's angry voice preceded him as he appeared from the kitchen, steaming coffee cup in his hand.

"I'll do no such thing." Bettina glared at him. "This has nothing to do with you, Mr. Mooring."

"It does if you're questioning Julie's ability to care for her son."

"I'm not questioning her abilities." Bettina eyes widened at the implication. "I just thought it might be difficult to send him back to that school after what happened. This school might give her peace of mind."

"Just go." Ben slammed the mug onto the table and coffee splattered the white silk scarf.

"How could you?" Bettina snatched up her scarf, eyeing the stain like a poisonous snake.

Julie stared at Ben—that was completely unnecessary, she had everything under control. He was either ignoring her or his glare-dar was on the fritz. Julie stood, and reached for the scarf. "I'm so sorry. Let me take that and see if I can remove the stain." She really did feel bad. Bettina might be horrible, but she'd come in good faith. And Ben was being a jerk.

Bettina shook her head and held the scarf closer. "I don't want you to ruin it. The kitchen is through here, correct? I need vinegar."

"Adam's in there. He can help you."

"Fine." Bettina disappeared through the doorway to the kitchen.

"Why did you do that?" Julie whispered to Ben, furious.

"I didn't spill it on purpose." Ben ran a hand through his hair. "She just drives me so crazy. The way she talks to you..."

Julie sighed, anger evaporating. Bettina drove her nuts, too, and okay, the way Bettina always talked to her was awful. She wrapped her arms around Ben and rested her head on his chest. "Thank you."

"Thank you?"

She pulled him closer. His heart thumped in her ear. "It's nice to have someone in my corner."

"I always want to be in your corner." His warm breath slid along her temple and the words warmed her to her toes.

Noise came from the kitchen and Cody ran through the opening to the living room, a typhoon of noise and action. "Hi, Mom." He dropped his bag, ran to Julie and grabbed her around the waist. She'd barely had time to step back from Ben. She was in heaven. Sandwiched between her two boys.

"You have a hockey game," Loraine called out as she followed him from the back of the house. "Go get your gear."

"Okay." Cody let go of Julie and bounced toward the side hallway.

"Only hockey gear!"

"I know, Grandma," Cody said as he disappeared, Loraine right behind him.

Julie leaned back into Ben. She was bursting—bursting with love. Cody was a force of nature. And she loved nature. There was something about everyone being safe that made her heart swell.

Somebody knocked on the front door.

Julie wanted to sigh. She was trying to enjoy a happy little hug with Ben, enjoy the calm after the storm, but the world was conspiring against her. "I'll get it."

"It's popular around here today."

"Yeah." Julie opened the door.

A woman in a fitted black suit and a collared white

shirt stood outside, blonde hair pulled severely back from her face. "I'm Bettina Wilcox's driver. She told me to remind her when it was time for her appointment."

"She's dealing with a scarf issue." Julie opened the door. "Come on in. She might be a few minutes."

"I can wait in the car."

Driving for Bettina probably meant the driver wasn't allowed to be seen or heard. The rich got weird about stuff like that. Not the rich—Bettina.

"Please, come on in and wait for her inside."

"I don't want to impose." The driver shifted uneasily. "If you can just tell her I knocked."

"Are you sure?" Julie opened the door wide.

"Mommy Bridgette?" Cody said behind her, and Julie's heart stopped.

Mommy. Bridgette. The woman that took her son.

Part of Julie refused to believe it. But the guilt and panic on the woman's face made it pretty clear she knew she'd been caught.

"My scarf is ruined," Bettina announced. "Mr. Mooring, I do hope you will be reimbursing me."

Cody said, "You called on the phone."

Julie turned, reluctant to let Bridgette out of her sight.

"Excuse me?" Bettina glanced between Cody and the doorway. "I don't know what you are referring to."

"Who is that woman?" Julie asked Bettina, nodding to the driver frozen on the porch.

"She's my driver."

"Bridgette?"

"I don't know her name," Bettina snarled. "She's the help."

Bridgette turned on her heel and ran.

"Stop her!" Julie yelled as she bolted out the door after the woman.

CHAPTER TWENTY-ONE

BEN LAPPED Julie once they hit the path. "Adam!"

He needed a cop. He had no idea what to do with a perp once they were in custody. No idea what to do, period.

Bridgette reached the car and opened the passenger door. When she faced Ben, the gun in her hand glinted in the afternoon sun. "Step back."

Ben raised his hands just as Adam came up behind him.

"You don't want to do this," Adam said in his calm cop voice, hands at his sides. "You didn't cause bodily harm or request a ransom. It's not a class X felony. But if you shoot me, you are guaranteed to die in prison. It's not worth it."

"Shut up." Bridgette slammed the passenger door. "Stay back."

Adam stayed where he was. "No one's moving."

"What am I supposed to do?" The gun bobbed in Bridgette's hand.

"Turn yourself in and it'll all work out." Adam's voice stayed steady.

Nothing on Ben was steady at the moment.

"It won't." Bridgette aimed the gun at Adam.

Ben wanted to pounce on the woman. She'd kidnapped Cody. She'd made Julie cry and scared everyone they loved. He wanted answers, but he wanted that gun pointed away from Adam. "Wait. Wait. Let's talk about it. Why did you take Cody?"

"It wasn't my idea." The gun snapped toward Ben.

Shit. He raised his hands higher.

"Whose idea was it?" Adam inched closer once her attention moved to Ben.

"That bitch." Bridgette swiveled back and forth like a caged animal. "Stay back," she snapped, pointing the business end of the gun at Adam.

Ben needed Adam to keep Julie and Cody safe. Adam knew what he was doing. Adam could draw the gun at his hip. Ben just needed to make sure Adam was around to ensure this whole thing ended safely.

"Who made you do this?" Ben asked. "You're the victim here. Help us."

"Ms. Wilcox. She said I'd make enough money to get back home." Bridgette shook her head, her eyes closed. "Now stop talking."

Ben lunged, and Adam yelled "Don't" as he drew his gun.

That was all Ben saw before he tackled Bridgette. A gunshot rang in his ears and fire burned along his arm as she rolled and fought. But he wouldn't let go of her. Couldn't let go.

He couldn't let her get to Julie or Cody. Not again. He held tight, grunting when the butt of the gun hit his back. Using his left hand, he grappled for her arm, the gun, and hissed when the barrel singed his fingers. She screamed in his ear when someone pushed on Ben's back.

Ben peeled her fingers back and the gun hit the ground with a thud. He rolled to the side and grabbed the gun before scrambling to his feet. Switching hands, he trained the gun on Bridgette as Adam clicked the cuffs into place.

"You're under arrest," Adam said.

That's it? "Shouldn't you be reading her her rights?" Ben asked.

"That's only on TV." Adam helped Bridgette up and sat her down against the tire of his car. "We don't Mirandize until interrogation. Are you shot?"

The gun had gone off. Ben didn't think he'd been shot. His hand burned like a mother, though. He held up his hand and winced. "No."

Adam tapped and swiped at his phone before pressing it to his ear. "Detective Barrows, we have the kidnapper here at the house. She pulled a gun. Can you call Agent Laramie? We'll need a bus." The detective must have said something, and then Adam disconnected. "They're on their way."

"Tell them it wasn't my idea," Bridgette pleaded. "Ms. Wilcox wanted to take Cody to some fancy school in New York. She made me break in. She made me pick him up. Then all of the sudden she tells me to take him back to his school."

Ben stared at her. "Why?"

"I don't know. She said that the mother was ready to give up custody and that she'd be honoring some guy named Edward."

Edward. Jackass was messing with Julie from the grave. He had a gift. A deplorable, twisted gift to torture Julie no matter where he was.

A loud crash came from the house. Julie.

Ben's hand throbbed, but he didn't care. He had to get to Julie. He had to get inside.

<hr>

"WELL, I HAVE TO LEAVE."

"Like hell." Julie blocked Bettina's path to the door. "Why did your driver kidnap my son?"

"I have no idea. Maybe she needed money. Desperation will cause people to do appalling things."

"Then why did you call her?"

"Who said I called her?"

"Cody heard you."

"He's a child. How does he know what he heard?"

"He's gifted, right?"

"But he's still a child. Julie, you are being ridiculous." Bettina dodged around Julie. "I'm done with this."

"I'm not done with you." Julie grabbed for her arm just as Bettina shoved her. Off balance, Julie's foot caught on the hall table. Her arms windmilled as she fought to stay upright, and a lamp landed on the floor with a crash. Bettina darted for the front door.

"Mom!" Cody ran up behind Julie just as she grabbed Bettina's wrist. "Are you okay?"

"I'm fine." She took out her cell phone one-handed, shaking. "Go up to your room and stay there until I come to get you," she snapped.

Tears slid down Cody's cheeks as he ran up the stairs. His door slammed a second later. She felt bad about scaring him, but before she could wallow too much Ben burst in the front door, carrying a gun. "Are you okay?"

Where did the gun come from? "I'm fine," Julie lied.

Bettina ripped her arm away. "I need to leave."

"You're not going anywhere." Ben tapped the gun on his thigh. Didn't point it, but it was implied. Not that he needed to point it at Bettina. She wasn't the hardened criminal type. Although Julie didn't really know her at all, did she? She didn't think Bettina was the kidnapping type, either.

Bettina peered down her nose at Ben. "I don't know what is going on here, but I want no part of it."

Ben's smile was positively nasty. "What's going on is that your driver is singing like a canary. She's telling us all about your plans to kidnap Cody and send him to school in New York. Then, when you thought Julie would give up custody, you had her drop him off back at school."

Julie swiveled from Ben to Bettina, jaw dropping. "What? Why would I give up custody?"

"Why wouldn't you give up custody." Bettina huffed. "Emily heard you talking to Ben the day of the search. You're right. You can't keep him safe here."

The day she and Ben searched the forest. Emily had been there. Commiserating. She'd been nice. And she knew that—

"Emily had no idea what was going on." Bettina sighed. "I can practically read the confusion in your simple mind."

"But why?"

"I promised your father I'd make sure his grandson lived up to his potential."

"But the school in Chicago—"

"That school isn't good enough. He needs to be surrounded by positive influences," Bettina shifted her gaze from Julie to Ben. "You have to understand how good this would be for him. How good this would be for you. You and Ben could marry and Cody would come back for holidays. He'd be challenged and he'd have a chance to grow."

"Stop. Just stop." Julie was so tired. She didn't want to fight anymore. She was done. "My son is and always will be my son. And I will ensure that he is challenged. And loved. And not brought up in some cold, lonely campus without his family."

"I just—"

"I don't care what you just." Julie got up in her face. Bettina looked afraid. Good. She should be afraid. Of course, that could be because of the sirens in the distance. "I don't care what my father wanted or what you think is best. He's my son. And how dare you attempt to take him away from me."

Julie slapped her.

Long overdue.

Bettina's head snapped to the side. Her eyes bulged as she touched her cheek. Funny. Julie was shocked too. This whole thing was a mess.

Adam came in the door as the sirens neared and dulled. He reached for Bettina's wrist. "Bettina Wilcox, you're under arrest."

"Do we need to get the police involved?" Bettina jerked away, but Adam didn't let go. "We just wanted what's best for you and for Cody," she told Julie.

"If you wanted what's best for Cody you would have asked me." Julie motioned to Adam. "Take her away."

"You think this is over?" Bettina snarled. "My lawyers will fight this. I won't spend a day in jail."

Adam pulled her arms behind her back and cuffed her. "Why take Cody from school, when you could have just taken him from hockey practice or when Bridgette broke into Julie's house?"

"Bridgette was incompetent. She never listened. She'd had so many opportunities and messed them up each time."

Julie went cold. "So you admit you told her to kidnap Cody?" Bettina had someone break into their home? What kind of crazy does that? Probably the same kind of crazy that kidnaps a kid because of a promise to a dead man.

Bettina sniffed. "I admit nothing. None of this will hold up in court."

"Well," Adam pointed out, "I am an officer of the law."

On that cue, Detective Barrows and Agent Laramie walked in the door. Adam tipped his head toward Bettina. "This is for you. She admitted to conspiracy to kidnap."

"I want my lawyers," Bettina said.

"You'll get your phone call once we're done processing you." Barrows led her out the door.

Adam sighed. "She's not wrong. Her lawyers will have her out pretty damn quick."

Julie didn't want her out. She didn't want to look over her shoulder for the rest of her life. "What can we do?"

"First, we're going to get a restraining order. Second, we're going to get the company lawyer on this." Ben was already texting on his phone. Probably with said lawyer.

"I'll have Garret double check the pool house, and then you can move back in." Adam started texting on his phone. "But right now, I'm going with the police. I'll keep you posted."

"Thanks, Adam," Julie said. "For everything."

"You're family." Adam disappeared with the police cruisers.

"Mom?" Cody peered down the stairs.

"Cody." Julie held out her arms. "Are you okay?"

"I'm fine." He ran to Julie and hugged her before turning to Ben. "What happened to your hand?"

"I touched something hot." Blisters lined the fingers of Ben's left hand.

Julie's breath caught. "We should get you to a doctor."

"I could fix it." Cody moved closer, obviously intrigued.

Ben's smile made Julie's heart flutter. "Let's leave it to the professionals, buddy." And the three of them stepped outside as an ambulance pulled up.

EPILOGUE

THIRTEEN YEARS later

THE BACKYARD WAS COVERED in streamers. Cody's name was all over the place—*Congratulations Cody* and *Cody's Graduation*. It was kind of silly. Everyone knew they were here for his graduation. He'd helped his mom send out the invitations.

In a little while, the big yard between his grandma's house and the guest house would be filled with people. And in three months he'd be on his way to college.

He couldn't wait. He would finally be on his own. No hovering cop-uncles. No helicoptering mother. He was eighteen, but no one would know given how they all hovered.

"Cody, have you seen the salt and pepper?" Ben carried a plate of brats and burgers out of the house, followed by Uncle Adam and Uncle Joe.

"By the bar." Cody shook out a white tablecloth and laid it on one of the tables spread along the lawn.

"Let me help you." His mom came over and gave him a glare. She'd been giving him that look for the past few months—every time he brought up graduation or college.

"What?" Like he didn't know.

"I'm just going to miss you." It was the same thing. Over and over again.

"I'll miss you too." And he would. He'd never been alone before. Not like that.

She wrapped her arms around him. "I've never been without you for that long before."

"I'm going to college, Mom, not getting kidnapped."

She shook her head. "Not funny."

They said at some point they'd laugh about it. They were still waiting for that point. "Sorry, Mom."

She smiled as Aunt Brook wobbled into the back yard, looking like she was going to have her baby any minute. She and Uncle Joe had been trying for years, and this would be their first.

Cody jogged over and offered her a hand. "Can I help you?" She was supposed to be on bedrest for a geriatric pregnancy, but they weren't allowed to say those words when she was in the room. Bedrest and geriatric usually led to her blood pressure spiking and lots of swearing.

And here she was, carrying a large bowl of salad.

"Thank you, sweetheart. But I can still walk."

"I can at least take that." He eased the bowl out of her hands.

"Are you supposed to be walking at all?" Cody's mom took her life into her own hands asking that question. Or any questions. Pregnant Aunt Brook was scary.

The glare she shot at his mother said if she was able, she'd be eviscerated by lasers shooting from her eyes and Cody would be an orphan. As it was, Aunt Brook just dropped into a lawn chair.

"How's the baby's room coming along?" Cody asked her. She had a lot of time since she couldn't go in to work. If she stepped foot in the door of her law firm, her employees were under strict orders to call the Chicago PD—well, one cop in particular.

"It's all greens and yellows." Aunt Brook glowed.

Uncle Joe walked up with a bottle of water. "Are you thirsty?" He leaned down and kissed her cheek. She took the bottle and smiled.

A scream came from the pool a few feet away, and Aunt Allison dropped into the chair next to her sister, calling out, "John Herbert and Sandra Loraine, do not fight." She made a face at her sister. "Are you sure you don't want those two? They got a few years on them, but you wouldn't have to do the pregnancy thing anymore."

"Stop trying to give our kids away." Uncle Adam sat on the other side of Aunt Allison and reached across for her hand.

"Ours fight."

"But they're also pretty good kids." Uncle Adam nodded toward the pool, where the kids splashed and laughed.

"True." Aunt Allison leaned back. "How are you feeling?"

"One more month." Aunt Brook took a drink from her water bottle.

"Come on," Shay called out as she and her husband Garret joined the group, "pop he-she out so you can come to the wedding."

"Wedding plans still on track?" Brook asked.

"It's hard to plan anything with Nip's fiancé in New York, but they're both coming next week since Gran can't travel."

"I can travel just fine," Gran muttered, poking a finger at Shay. "Some moron gets a degree and everyone thinks they know what they're talking about."

Shay sighed. "It's not some moron, it's your doctor, Gran."

"Ach, he's a moron." Gran lowered herself into a chair underneath an umbrella. "He won't let me do anything."

Grandma Loraine sat next to her. "These kids won't let me use the bathroom alone." She was exaggerating, sort of. She had a bad fall a couple years ago, and made everybody nervous.

"Where's Dale?" Ben asked.

Dad had really stepped up over the past few years. He was dating a woman, who might actually stick this time. Hopefully this one wouldn't want Cody to call her mom.

"Where's the diploma?" Shay asked Cody.

Cody went and got it. He flipped the cover open with a grin.

"Cody Byrnes," Shay read. "Congratulations."

When his mom married Ben, she changed her last name from Connolly to Mooring. Cody had decided to honor his biological father's family and Grandma Loraine by taking their name.

But the man who'd been there for him since the beginning had always been Ben.

"We're going to miss you, kid." Ben bumped his shoulder with his own. Together, they looked over the party. Everyone playing and laughing.

"I'll miss you all too." And Cody was going to miss this. His family. They'd been through a lot together, but they always managed to come out on top. And with them behind him, he could take on the world.

EXTRAS

Thank you for supporting an independent author. It would be great if you could leave a review or a rating wherever you purchased this book, or on Goodreads.

Would you like to know when my next book is available? You can sign up for my new release email list at http://www.vanessamknight.com or like my Facebook page at http://facebook.com/vanessamknightauthor.

ABOUT THE AUTHOR

Vanessa M. Knight has always enjoyed writing, and once she found mystery and romance, she was addicted. She props her laptop in the suburbs of Chicago with her family and menagerie of four-pawed claw-babies (AKA cats and dogs.) That laptop has partnered-in-crime to write contemporary romances with a dash of humor and splash of snark.

When she has a few moments to spare, you can find her singing off-key (but she assures everyone it's still considered singing), reading, kickboxing, or killing a few brain cells as she stares at the many sitcoms and dramas available through the Internet and TV.

For more information on Vanessa, including her Internet haunts, contest updates, and details on her upcoming novels, please visit her website at www.-vanessamknight.com.

Chicago's Finest Series

Second Time's the Charm

Stark Raving Mad

Stealing Vegas

Final Strike

Busted Series

Busting In

Busting Out

Busting Through

And look for her Contemporary New Adult series:

Ritter University Series

Major Renovations

What Happens in College...

Christmas Breakdown

Rushing In

Sophomore Slump

The Make-up Test